GREEN-TIMBER TRAILS

A weasel in its winter ermine, held in the first trap, occupied him for a few minutes

GREEN-TIMBER TRAILS

Wild Animal Stories
of the North Country

A Nature Classic
by

WILLIAM
GERARD
CHAPMAN

Foreword by Peter A. A. Berle
President, National Audubon Society
◆

Illustrations by Paul Bransom
and Charles Livingston Bull

The Countryman Press
Woodstock, Vermont

Countryman Classics are books of eloquence, charm, and literary quality that our editors wish to restore to print in affordable new editions, for the enjoyment of successive generations of readers.

© 1918, 1919 by the Century Co., 1947 by Gerard Chapman. Foreword © 1991 by Peter A. A. Berle.

Green-Timber Trails was originally published in 1919 by The Century Company. The illustrations by Paul Bransom and Charles Livingston Bull are from the original edition.

This edition is printed in 1992 by the Countryman Press, Inc., P.O. Box 175, Woodstock, Vermont 05091.

Library of Congress Cataloging-in-Publication Data

Chapman, William Gerard, 1877-1945.
    Green-timber trails: wild animal stories of the north country: a
nature classic / by William Gerard Chapman; foreword by Peter
A. A. Berle; illustrations by Paul Bransom and Charles Livingston Bull.
        p.   cm.
    Originally published: New York: Century Co., 1919.
    ISBN 0-88150-240-5 : $13.00
    1. Adventure stories, American.   2. Outdoor life—Fiction.
    3. Animals—Fiction.   I. Title.
PS3505.H427G7   1992
813'.52—dc20   92-26041
                                                                      CIP

Cover design by James F. Brisson
Printed in the United States of America on recycled paper
10 9 8 7 6 5 4 3 2 1

CONTENTS

Foreword

William Gerard Chapman's *Green-Timber Trails*, first
published in 1919, is a collection of adventure stories that
takes us back to a less complicated time. Chapman's
protagonists—bucks, loons, bears, wolverines and trappers—struggle with one another for survival in the great
north woods. Men are trappers and woodsmen. Women
are spunky young homebodies who wear calico skirts and
are prone to being cornered by bears. Agility, muscle and
luck determine who lives and dies as predator and prey
pursue their natural instincts. Animals have anthropomor-
phic emotions, and principles of rough justice govern
conduct. Thus, "Scarside" Buck, befriended as an abandoned fawn by a child, later saves the boy from a panther
attack. Woodsman Dave prevents his colleague from
killing a bear. Injured and freezing, Dave had crawled into
the den of the hibernating beast. Its body warmth had kept
him alive and when Dave's turn comes, he saves his furry
benefactor. The wolverine, which repeatedly steals from a
trapline, breaks into the trapper's cabin and sets it ablaze
after falling into the embers in the fireplace. It still earns
the trapper's respect, even though it bested him at every
encounter.

Modern wildlife biologists define and interpret animal behavior differently today. But stories of adventure and danger which arose at a time when the perception existed that humans and beasts competed with each other and natural forces on more or less equal terms are part of the heritage of a nation which subdued a wild frontier.

Instinct for survival spurred humankind to seek dominion over all surroundings. The woodsmen in *Green-Timber Trails* did not have time to consider that their activities would eliminate the forest and wildlife that defined their existence. Today we are similarly blind as we eliminate the remaining ancient forests, dam our wild rivers, and imperil the atmosphere.

Today our well-being will be determined by our ability to translate respect for the noble qualities of the beast, exhibited by Chapman and his frontiersmen, to respect for the air, soil, water, and habitat upon which we and wildlife depend. Our survival is still at stake but the challenge now is to foster nature, not subdue it.

Peter A. A. Berle
President
National Audubon Society

Coming across an almost unknown work of excep-
tional literary quality is one of the rarest and most exciting
events in the life of a publisher. Over a year ago, Gerard
Chapman sent us a copy of his father's sole book, *Green-
Timber Trails*, published in 1919, and it soon became
obvious to us that this long-forgotten book was one of
those rare events. We at The Countryman Press were
immediately captivated by Chapman's spare but polished
style, the skillful construction of his stories, and the
extraordinary sensitivity to wildlife and nature underlying
them.

To double-check our judgment, we tried *Green-Timber
Trails* out on a variety of discerning readers, ranging in age
from early teens to early sixties. The response was unani-
mous—this was a book we *must* bring back into print.
Clearly, although almost forgotten today, Chapman was a
writer in the tradition of—and on a par with—Ernest
Thompson Seton and the other renowned nature writers
of the early Twentieth Century.

William Gerard Chapman (1877-1945) was a remarkable figure in many ways. His formal education
extended only through high school, and his command of

the English language seems to have been acquired through his avid reading of such masters of English prose as Dickens, Pepys, Galsworthy, and Thackeray. Although raised in Brooklyn, New York, Chapman spent summers as a youth on a farm in Ulster County, New York, where his love of nature and the outdoors was nurtured.

For most of his adult life, Chapman was a prominent publisher and literary agent in Chicago. At the same time, he contributed stories and verse to some of the most respected American and British magazines of the time and even wrote lyrics for songs. Chapman was also an avid outdoorsman and student of nature, who loved to camp, fish, and hunt in the then wilderness areas of Wisconsin and northern Ontario. On these expeditions, he observed the behavior of wildlife and found inspiration for stories such as those collected in *Green-Timber Trails*.

Chapman's nature stories attracted widespread critical acclaim and were included in anthologies edited by the dean of early Twentieth Century nature writers, Ernest Thompson Seton, and by the eminent historian Henry Steele Commager. When *Green-Timber Trails* appeared, it was warmly praised by reviewers in the nation's leading papers and magazines—the *Chicago Tribune, New York Tribune, Cleveland Plain-Dealer, St. Louis Post-Dispatch,* and *Sports Afield,* to name just a few.

We at The Countryman Press feel honored to have the opportunity to reissue these remarkable and enduring nature stories and hope that our readers will treasure them as much as we have.

THE SWIFTWATER BUCK

GREEN-TIMBER TRAILS

THE SWIFTWATER BUCK

A CROSS the sunlit swale came stalking cautiously a whitetail doe with her five-months fawn stepping daintily at her side, the weanling showing a curious, long, whitish scar on its flank. Before emerging from the dark recesses of the wood they had stood in the spruce tangle at the forest's edge for several minutes, the doe searching the open with eyes and nose and ears, her fawn as motionless as herself in obedience to an unspoken command. No evidence of an enemy coming to the mother's alert senses, the strained attitude of the two deer relaxed and they broke quietly through the leafy screen. While the care-free youngling, under the influence of the genial warmth, capered joyously about the heels of its mother, secure in its faith in her guardian-

3

ship, the doe's vigilance remained unabated. All during their excursion into the border-land that lay between ancient forest and rudely cultivated ground she sniffed at each puff of air and weighed every rustle of grass, while her eyes sought for telltale motions that might betray a seeming bush or rock or tree-bole as some animate danger from which to flee.

The mother deer was in mighty fear of humankind, but it is doubtful if the fawn would have evidenced any great terror had one of the tribe appeared, for the same recent experience from which sprung the doe's overpowering dread of man had left the fawn with as great a curiosity concerning him. Early in the spring the doe, driven by wolves, had in her extremity leaped among the pasturing herd of a settler; and the cattle, alarmed by her abrupt advent and catching the fever of her fear, had raced to the barn-yard. The doe, tolled along by the rush, soon found herself in a strange fenced enclosure, and falling exhausted from her terrific effort had been captured and imprisoned within a calf-pen by the backwoods farmer. The farmer had acted on impulse, and once the deer was confined he wondered what he would do with her, his first thought naturally being of the venison she would provide for his table. But the evidence of her approaching maternity stayed his hand, and his entranced young son settled the question by demanding her as his own possession, believing she would prove the most wonderful playmate a boy ever had.

The next day the boy, coming early to the pen to feed and make overtures to the captive, was transported by the discovery that a baby deer had arrived during the night. Henceforth he devoted himself to cultivating the friendship of the tiny milk-spotted fawn.

During the brief period of her captivity the mother deer remained as wild and unapproachable as she had become once the exhaustion of her flight had passed; indeed, she seemed to grow wilder as the narrowness of her quarters wore upon her freedom-loving spirit. But to her dismay she was unable to impress upon the elfin wilding at her side the dangerous quali-

5

ties of the man creatures who came to view them through the pole walls of their prison. True, the larger of the enemies poked very appetizing provender into the pen and set pails of water within easy-reaching distance; and of these she finally partook in the interest of her baby, after long refusal of them began to lessen the supply of its nourishment. The fawn, wilfully unmindful of her distressed cautionings, poked an inquiring moist muzzle against the small fingers that stretched toward him through the openings. The childish voice that invited him to playfellowship brought no fear to his guileless heart, and even the harsher voice of the bearded giant who came now and then gave him no more than a tremor of distrust that quickly lost itself in fascinated wonder. Perhaps the untutored baby heart sensed the kindly note in the gruff tones to which his mother, sophisticated in the ways of man, was deaf.

Only for a few days did the situation endure. One morning the boy, peering into the pen, was cut short in his salutations by the

sight of a red gash in the flank of the baby
deer. The fawn had torn his side deeply but
not dangerously on a protruding splinter, and
the crimsoned streak in his delicate coat smote
the child's heart with horror and sympathy.
Casting previous admonitions to the winds, the
little boy lifted the latch of the pen door, which
could be fastened only on the outside, and ran
to the fawn to comfort his wounded protégé.
The doe backed into the far corner, trembling
with terror, then suddenly sprang for the
opening, bowling the child over in her rush.
At her bleat of command the fawn dashed
after her, maternal authority overcoming
whatever of reluctance he may have felt in
deserting the sociable little two-legged animal;
and the boy, rising bewildered and with the
hot tears springing to his eyes, emerged from
the pen just in time to glimpse the two grace-
fully leaping forms disappearing over the crest
of a rise in mid-pasture. With her white flag
guiding the youngling, the freed mother deer
streaked for the friendly cover that loomed
invitingly before her eyes, and quickly doe and

7

fawn were swallowed up in the cool, dim sanctuary of the forest.

On the occasion of the whitetails' venture into the open no untoward signs disturbed the serenity of the golden October afternoon. The untainted air, heavy with spicy odors of late wild flowers and fruiting shrubs, vibrated only to the drowsy rasp of cicadas, the notes of winging birds, and the occasional booming of frogs from the marshy dip of land in which the swale lost itself a little beyond.

At the far side of the swale, where the ground tipped slightly upward, a straggling thicket of hazel and hawthorn fringed the tilth of a backwoods settlement. It was this luxuriant growth that drew the doe from the gloomy coverts of the wood to browse on the fruit that hung in rich profusion from the interlacing branches. The fuzz-coated hazel-nuts were as yet untouched by frost and their green succulence appealed mightily to her wild palate; and the tiny red haw "apples" that stippled the glossy green leafage with glowing

8

scarlet had a spicy tang at this season that even her mother prudence could not resist.

She knew the dangers attendant upon foraging this region, for on the other side of the wild hedge lay cultivated fields; and experience warned her that wherever the earth had been ravaged of its trees by the ruthless humankind the spoilers were wont to appear disconcertingly at any hour of the day. Night was the ordained time for taking toll of this out-flung strip of cover, but the aromatic fragrance of its ripening fruit had penetrated the forest on the autumn zephyrs and she could not resist its allure. Had she known it, she was in little danger of interruption by man this day, for the crop of the adjacent field had been cut, and the sear yellow shocks of corn and array of golden-cheeked pumpkins that dotted the russet earth about them had been left for the first early frosts to temper and sweeten, while the farmer folk pursued their activities elsewhere.

The doe fell to the feast and the fawn soon followed her example, finding the tender nuts and red haws of a new and captivating flavor; and the two fed greedily on the delicious fare until with dulled appetites they were content to nibble here and there fastidiously, wherever a particularly tempting cluster drew the attention.

Ever that which is just out of reach is the most to be desired, and the doe coveted the red-gleaming haws that hung in the upper branches beyond the utmost stretching of her neck. But she would have them, and rising on her hind-feet she sought the fruit with her eager, curling tongue. She could not maintain this position for more than a few seconds, however, and the effort was not wholly successful. So she supported herself by placing her fore-feet against the slender trunk of the tree and by straining upward managed to gather some of the high-hanging fruit.

Satisfied with her success, she started to drop to the ground, but one hoof slipped into the fork where a branch left the parent stem, and the sudden downpull wedged it tight. The unexpected wrench threw her off her balance and she swung half around, the bone of her leg breaking, and hung in mid-air with her back to the sward, impotent to free herself.

At her sudden snort of dismay and agony the fawn stiffened into alert watchfulness; then as he saw the astonishing posture of his mother and sensed that she was in trouble, he bleated in frightened inquiry and rushed up to her. But she did not move from her strange pose to comfort him with licking tongue and soft breathings of reassurance, as was her wont when his fear was aroused. Instead, the breath rattled in her throat terrifyingly, and her eyes, after one mute appealing glance into his own, lost their familiar look of mother-love in a mad gleam of anguish.

The fawn nuzzled her soft neck that drooped backward until the head nearly touched the ground, but the only response to his caress was a violent writhing of the stricken body as the doe made one last despairing effort to regain an upright position. Then with strength sapped by pain and terror she hung limp and still, and her eyes slowly glazed as her wild heart broke.

While the slowly westering sun pursued its journey across the blue expanse the fawn strove to awaken some evidence of life in the strangely inanimate form of his mother. He circled the stiffening frame again and again, occasionally withdrawing a short distance and prancing back to bunt playfully at the maternal sides, expecting the customary attention to his sallies; but all his attempts to win recognition were in vain. His heart slowly became charged with a vague uneasiness as his wistful efforts brought only a slight swaying of the body that seemed so distressingly cold and unresponsive.

The long, unhappy afternoon waned and as the sun dropped beyond the black-green rampart of trees a chill crept into the air with the sudden twilight. The fawn pressed close to the yielding flank of the doe, seeking warmth and protection from the unknown dangers that surely lurked here in the unfamiliar open once the brightness of day was dimmed. Never before had nightfall found him elsewhere than in some friendly covert in the heart of the forest, in comforting nearness to his mother; and this inexplicable lack of solicitude for his welfare increased his puzzlement and distress.

At the height of his misery a snapping of twigs at the forest's edge caused his heart to palpitate with a new dread. He sprang quivering to attention, eyes gazing fearsomely in the direction of the sound, ears alert for parental guidance. He saw a dim, lumbering form emerge from the gloom and take its way across the open, a cautious sniffing proclaiming its interest in what lay beyond in the shadow of the hedge.

Suddenly the intruder rushed forward, and still the expected command did not come. In a tremor of indecision the fawn waited until the hulking black shape was almost upon him; then discretion luckily overcame the influence of training. With a bleat of fear he forsook the side of his indifferent mother and darted down the swale and into the enveloping blackness of the wood as the big bear, disdaining the fleeing fawn, plunged toward the suspended body of the doe and struck it down with a vicious sweep of his paw.

Thus was the baby whitetail buck orphaned and driven to pit his slight strength and store of knowledge against a hostile wilderness. When the plunging black demon, whose dangerous presence his mother already had taught him to avoid, had frightened him into flight, he ran deep into the forest until his slender legs could no longer carry him; and sinking down in a copse of low-growing spruce he rested in trembling fear through the night. The nocturnal prowlers whose soft-footed activities occasionally broke upon his sensitive hearing kept his little heart in a flutter of fear; but chance or a well-selected refuge served him well, and he was not molested during the long dark hours. When morning streaked the forest floor with its first gray shafts of light he timidly drew out of his shelter and nibbled at the sparse grass and tenderer leaves within his reach. He fed sparingly, for his dread of the unknown, made poignant by loneliness, kept him in a continual state of apprehension over each tiny sound of the life that surrounded him. The dew on the grass and leaves satisfied his thirst, and he kept within a small area while he breakfasted, returning to his haven beneath the screening spruce foliage as the sun rose higher and flooded the tree-girt aisles of the wood with a more searching radiance.

Here he cowered as the morning wore on, open-eared for the softly questioning murmur of his mother, which he awaited with still unimpaired confidence. Once she had awakened from her strange apathy and exerted herself to escape from the dimly comprehended peril that to him already was only a fading memory, she would come to search him out. Always she had come when his lonely wait grew irksome, as he crouched in some artfully chosen hiding-place while she foraged, even as she would come now. A twig snapped, and as his startled eyes sought the cause, they rested on a familiar form that suddenly loomed before him almost at the edge of the tangle in

which he lay hidden, and which of a certainty
was the mother for whom he yearned. But
as he eagerly rose to his feet two fawns came
into view behind her. The puzzle of this
stiffened him in his tracks, and something
caused the new-comers to stiffen likewise at
the same instant, their gaze, however, passing
beyond his covert. For a tense moment the
tableau held; then out of the corner of his eye
the fawn glimpsed a thick-furred shadowy
shape that was creeping toward him through
the underbrush. He turned a panic-stricken
gaze upon it, and a trembling seized him
as the evil-appearing creature drew swiftly
nearer.

The hungry, glowering eyes of a prowling
lynx had penetrated the tangle and espied the
hiding young deer, and the ugly cat had approached soundlessly almost within springing-
distance. The paralysis of fear held the fawn
rigid as the lynx crouched only a few feet
beyond the edge of the copse; then, just as it
loosed itself for the spring, the tension broke
and with a bleat of terror he tore through the

yielding wall, escaping by a hair's breadth the savagely spread claws that descended where he had stood.

The leap of the baby buck was in the direction of the others of his kind, who at the bursting into view of both lynx and fawn sprang into flight. He joined them, and the little company sped through the mazes of the forest away from the dreaded enemy; while the thwarted lynx, after a few ineffectual and half-hearted leaps toward them, glared malignantly after the fleeing forms, and snarling his rageful disappointment slunk off through the trees on a quest for easier game.

However narrow the escape of the forest folk from danger, once they are free of it their normal calm returns quickly and memory of the incident mercifully fades; though doubtless the faint impress that may be left is added to the store of accumulated experience that blossoms finally into instinct. Were it not for this evanescent quality of their emotions the lives of the wildings would be a never-ending tragedy of racking terror. The little band of deer, their hearts at first wildly palpitant with fright at the onslaught of the lynx, soon slowed their rush, and at the distance of a mile or less came to a halt in a grove of young aspen and birch on the slope of a hill and quietly began to feed, with hardly a thought of their late experience. Albeit the mother doe pursued her invariable custom of keeping a careful watch with all her senses.

The new-comer in their ranks seemingly gave the mother deer little concern. His having joined them in the common race from danger was perhaps a sufficient claim upon relationship; and there was now no troublesome consideration of another mouth to feed, for all three youngsters had been weaned with the shedding of their spotted coats in September. The two fawns displayed a trifle of curiosity over the self-adopted one's scent, which assuredly was not that of their own family; but a few bunting-contests in which the new brother amply held his own soon established him as a worthy member of the group.

The lonely heart of the little orphan was

lonely no longer. In a very short space he forgot his troubles—and his mother as well, it must be admitted—and merged his life into that of his companions. And lucky it was for him that this was possible, for otherwise he hardly could have survived long against the savage marauders of the forest; nor, had he been miraculously successful in this, could he have lived through the long, pitiless winter that soon was to descend upon the land, without the wit and sagacity of an older deer to aid him.

As the crisp, cold days of early winter arrived the little family was joined by a lordly buck, who calmly assumed leadership over them. His attitude toward the younglings was indifferent, but he nevertheless was ready to resent any intrusion upon the family circle, even by others of his own clan. During this period they fed luxuriously upon the rich mast of oak and beech and laid up fat against the scant fare of approaching winter. With the coming of snow the leader lost much of his arrogance, and when it grew deep and the bitter gales came whistling down from the far Arctic reaches he led them into the densest timber of the region, to which other groups were converging; and here a band composed of several families made common cause and established themselves in an immense "yard." This was a labyrinth of trampled paths among the trees, providing a haven from enemies and enabling them to reach the twigs and bark of the surrounding low growth and the dried grass and moss beneath the snow blanket.

On this slender diet they managed to survive the harsh period of cold, but it was little better than starvation and the melting snows found them lean to emaciation. Long before spring had broken the iron seal of winter the elder bucks—sorry, scraggy figures with ribs protruding, their lordliness gone with their shed antlers—drifted out of the colony, and the does and the younger deer were left to keep house alone until released by the warm south winds. When the snow had melted from the exposed places they broke out of their desolate runs and sought the tender sprouts of grass and early plant life that sprang fairylike out of the brown earth; and these and the juicy shooting buds of trees and shrubs soon wrought a transformation in their shrunken, shabby appearance. With this improved nourishment they shed their winter coats of coarse grayish blue and donned a sightlier garb of sleek light brown that glistened with pale red tints when a now friendlier sun caressed them in the greening glades.

Spring drew on apace and the young buck's foster-mother evinced a desire for seclusion from her family, emerging later with a pair of tiny milk-spotted fawns. These new arrivals supplanted the yearlings in her affections, though for the present the family group remained intact. While she would not brook the older members' presence during the first month of the twins' life, they all held to the same locality and generally drew together at the drinking-hour. She grew less reserved when the babies had acquired a measure of strength and the agility to evade the occasional playful onslaughts of their elder sisters and brother. Together the little band ranged and fed and slept as the days lengthened and warmed into the balmy summer-time.

The young buck at this period began to feel restless. He was stirred by a longing to free himself from the ties of family and to explore his forest world unhampered by tagging relatives. The tiny "spikes" that were now appearing filled him with pride and a spirit of independence that one day led him to wander far from the family circle and forget to return at drinking-time. Instead he sought the margin of a wild little lake a long distance from his accustomed range, and here he slaked his thirst and then lay down in a cool alder thicket to chew his cud and drowse away the afternoon hours with no thought of return to the fold.

The severing of old associations was complete. Henceforth he was to break his own wilderness trails, having survived the perils of early infancy and fallen by good chance, when orphaned, under the training of the wise old foster-mother.

THE SWIFTWATER BUCK

The scar-sided buck in a few years achieved a reputation in the settlements beyond that of any of his fellows. Known and recognized both by the livid mark on his right flank and the immense size to which he had grown, he became famous throughout the Swiftwater country. He was credited with possessing either uncanny craft or the gift of uncommonly good luck, for no magnificently antlered head was more coveted, or more assiduously hunted, than the one that reared itself proudly on his broad, powerful shoulders. And frequently something more than desire to possess the finest head they had known inspired the efforts of the hunters of the region. His depredations on the fields and truck patches of the scattered farmsteads periodically sent irate backwoods farmers on his trail vowing to exterminate this despoiler of their crops. But these usually returned without having seen the big buck; or else if they caught a glimpse of him he got himself so swiftly out of sight that no chance offered for a successful shot.

23

That the buck knew the difference between a man unarmed and a man with a gun was an opinion shrewdly held by one young hunter, who kept this view to himself for reasons of his own. Probably some early experience in being creased by a bullet from one of those fire-spouting, loud-voiced sticks that men sometimes carried had put an idea into the buck's head. Dogs did not seem to excite any great terror in him, and on numerous occasions he had turned on those that followed his trail and driven them off. But usually he accepted the challenge and gave them an exhilarating run, and when the game palled, broke his trail craftily and left the dogs to plod back home foot-sore and chop-fallen.

It should be said, however, in justice to the best shots of the region, that there were occasions when something besides craft or luck saved him. For certain long-headed hunters saw in the sparing of the big buck a promise of larger deer in the Swiftwater country; and in the interests of a sturdier strain and better hunting many a trigger-finger was stayed when the sight held temptingly against the smooth dun of his shoulder.

The history of Old Scarside, the name by which the great buck came to be known, was familiar to the settlement folk. Laban Knowles, the farmer who had imprisoned the doe who bore him, and his son Lonny held themselves his sponsors; indeed, Lonny maintained that the buck belonged to him, and always was driven to white anger by the often-expressed designs on the deer's life.

Lonny desired above all things that his big buck deer, who only a few years before had plainly shown his willingness to be friends with him, should live unharmed. Old Scarside, magnificent and storied buck whitetail of the Swiftwater country, had responded to his voice and nuzzled his hand when he and Lonny were hardly more than babies! The intimate association unfortunately had been terminated after all too brief a life, else surely it would have progressed to a thorough understanding; but the friendship begun still held with one of the parties to it, and Lonny's assump-

tion of proprietorship in the biggest deer of
the region was known to all the inhabitants of
the border country. Some there were who
presumed upon this attitude to torment the lad
with threats to bring down the monarch of the
hunting-grounds; but doubtless it had its share
in preserving the buck against some of the
gruff old pioneers who still retained a kinship
with boys. There were deer a-plenty to be
had for the shooting; why break the heart of
a promising young hunter who certainly had
some claim on the clever antlered rascal?

Lonny Knowles was by way of becoming a
top-notch woodsman, and his skill as a marksman with his twenty-two rifle was a matter of
note among his fellows. Whenever his farm
duties permitted he roamed the woods, shooting what small game was needed for the home
table, but finding his greatest pleasure in
studying the wild life of the great timbered
stretches that enclosed the settlement. Of all
the wildwood folk the scar-sided whitetail
deer held first place in his interest. Noiselessly
he ranged the feeding-grounds and runways

that he had come to know were used by "his buck," and often his careful stalking was rewarded by a sight of the noble animal. His great wish was to overcome the buck's instinctive fear, in the boyish hope that eventually he would succeed in reëstablishing an understanding with his one-time friend. And very patiently and persistently he sought to accustom the buck to his presence. Whenever he came upon his track, easily distinguished by its size, he trailed him with the silent efficiency of an Indian. When finally Old Scarside was sighted, Lonny drew as near to him as cover and wind permitted and watched him long and admiringly. Then, leaving his rifle on the ground, he would silently rise and show himself, all his movements quiet and restrained and his manner casual. Up would come the buck's head with a snort of surprise at the sudden apparition. Usually he would bound away the instant Lonny showed himself. Sometimes, when Lonny stood forth while the buck's eyes were turned aside, Scarside would suddenly become aware of an alien figure standing astonishingly close, where no figure had been an instant before; and snorting and stamping petulantly, with eyes and nose would seek to penetrate the mystery. Then, suspicion overcoming curiosity, he would wheel and plunge swiftly from the spot.

But gradually, very gradually, the painstaking methods of the young woodsman began to have their effect on the buck. The casual approach, unthreatening manner, and eyes that never fixed themselves disquietingly upon his own, were strangely at variance with what his experience had taught him of the ways of the man tribe, though sometimes the evidence carried on a veering puff of wind would unmistakably proclaim the intruder a member of it. And as time went on a growing familiarity with this seemingly harmless individual, smaller in stature than his other persecutors and never bearing that abhorrent instrument of noise and flame associated with these enemies, slowly wore down the fine edge of his fear. Often he would stand and stamp and snort for minutes, merely backing off slowly as Lonny advanced upon him inch by inch. Then as a quiver of muscles rippled the sheen of his coat and signaled a break for cover, Lonny would stay him with a bleated "Mah!" And for an instant longer the wondering buck would tarry, to puzzle out the meaning of this, before discretion sent him bounding away into the green forest depths. Later, when the buck's departure was still longer delayed, Lonny would utter soothing words to him:

"You ain't afeared o' me, are you, old feller? 'Member when you an' me was babies, you licked my hand. We're friends still, ain't we? Now, don't git skeery an' cut an' run. I ain't a-goin' to bite you!"

Awed and fascinated by the softly spoken words, Scarside would stand a-quiver, then run back a few steps and halt half hidden in a near-by thicket, pawing and whistling, his big liquid eyes never leaving this strangely ingratiating one of the enemy kind. In the dim recesses of his brain did some faint memory stir at the voice that in the first days of his life spoke to him in the universal language of infant brotherhood? Or perhaps some remnant of that early curiosity of his concerning man creatures remained to weaken the ancestral dread.

His whistling Lonny chose to interpret as a reply to his own remarks.

"Remember, do you! Well, then, don't be so bashful. I ain't never a-goin' to hurt you, Old Scarside. It's all along o' that scar that you got away from me when you was jest a little feller. You ain't forgotten, have you?— Well, good-by then, if you're a-goin'."

When Lonny described his adventures in friendliness with the deer, Laban scoffed amusedly at his son's firm belief in Scarside's memory of the early incident.

"A deer hain't got no memory, don't you ever believe it! He's jest gittin' used to you an' your quiet ways, like any wild critter will ef you show yourself often enough an' don't pay special attention to 'em at first. He's jest curious about you, an' a deer's as curious a critter as any woman.

"But ef he's your deer, like you claim, you

better learn him to keep out o' the clearin's,"
Laban continued, his whimsical tone changing
to half-angry seriousness as he thought of the
devastated field of rutabagas he had just
visited. "The pesky critter's gittin' to be a
blame nuisance, eatin' up half the crops. Last
night he liked to spile the hull 'baga patch,
tromplin' what he did n't eat. I ain't a-goin'
to stand him much longer. Ef he don't quit
ruinin' the fields I 'll put a bullet inter his big
carcass!"

"Don't you never do it, Pa!" burst out
Lonny. "He's only takin' what he thinks is
rightly his'n, an' we oughter be able to spare
a few 'bagas an' such like. He *is* my deer, and
I won't stand to have him hurted!"

Laban grumbled in his throat and turned
away. The generous-hearted farmer was
troubled by the knowledge that Old Scarside's
continued depredations had reached the un-
bearable stage. Fences were as nothing to the
big creature, and his despoiling of growing
crops was now a matter of almost nightly oc-
currence. The countryside was becoming in-

flamed against the buck, who left his sign manual in each invaded area in the form of tracks that in size resembled those of a calf.

Leaving the boy protesting against the threat, Laban strode off on his way to a neighbor's to assist in raising a new barn-frame. A short cut could be made by paddling across the lake that lay between the farmsteads, the trail to this leading over a hardwood ridge beyond which stretched the broad sheet of water. On the shelving beach his birch-bark lay among the bushes, and noting as he shoved it in that a stiff breeze was blowing in his face, he decided to weight the bow with a small rock. Otherwise the light craft would expose so much free-board to the gale that he would have difficulty in keeping its prow in the wind's eye. Bending forward, he was about to deposit the rock carefully in the canoe when his design was rudely frustrated. His next conscious thought was that the Wendigo—that demon of Northern Indian legend which seizes men in its talons and bears them off on torturous journeys through space—had

savagely snatched at him and sent him whirling dizzily through the air.

Back in the timber of the ridge a big, nobly
antlered buck deer, the pride—and bane—
of the Swiftwater country, had watched the
striding man with arrogant eyes, eyes that for
the moment held no glint of fear. The fever
of the sweethearting time was in his blood this
crisp November morning, and dread of man
was forgotten in the swift anger that blazed
within him when his trysting was disturbed. Stiffly he stood for a moment in his
screen of bushy hemlock, neck swollen with
the madness in his veins, bloodshot eyes glaring upon the unsuspecting interloper. Then,
intent upon vengeance, he followed after the
figure noisily descending the slope. His
progress was a series of prancing steps, though
his feet fell cunningly without sound, and he
shook his magnificent head threateningly as
he advanced.

He was only a few paces behind when the
man, reaching the shore, suddenly swerved to

look about; and he froze for a moment in expectation of the stare of those disconcerting eyes. But the man's gaze did not lift from the ground. He picked up something and turned his back again and bent over at the water's edge.

The opportunity was too tempting. The buck plunged forward, his lowered head aimed at the crouching figure, and drove at it with all the power of his hard-muscled body. The impact was terrific and the result startling, no less to the object of his attack than to the deer. For the man with a grunt of astonishment shot from the shore, turning upside down as he went, and out of the splash that followed emerged, not the man, but what appeared to be a smooth brown log that trembled and rolled crazily among the wavelets and gave forth weird muffled bellowings!

The backwoodsman, lifted into the air by the amazing assault from the rear, had let go the rock, which at the instant was poised above the canoe, as his hands instinctively reached for the gunwales. As he catapulted into the

lake, his grasp on the birch-bark turned it over
on him and he found himself upright in the
water, his face above the surface but in darkness. For a moment utter bewilderment
possessed him; then realizing that he was
standing in over five feet of freezing water,
his head in the hollow of his capsized canoe,
to which he still clung tenaciously, he burst
into language and sought to extricate himself.

With a wrench of his arms he threw the
canoe over and turned a wrathful glare toward
the bank. Hot indignation choked him momentarily as his eyes fell on the author of his
plight pawing the gravel and shaking his
antlers in invitation to combat. Then he
found his voice.

"Ye confounded, tarnation critter!" sputtered Laban, at a loss for adequate words with
which to express his feelings. "So 't was you
butted me into the lake! Ye'll pay fer this,
with a bullet through yer hide, afore ye're a
day older, ye scar-sided devil." He shook his
fist at the animal and started to scramble up

the steep bottom, continuing his abuse vigor-
ously. But half-way up he came to a stop,
perplexed. What would he do when he
reached the bank? The buck plainly was in
a fighting mood, and no unarmed man was a
match for those driving, keen-rimmed hoofs
and daggerlike antler points. Scarside stood
his ground, stamping and snorting and lowering his head in challenge.

Laban wondered angrily if he would have to
stand there waist-deep in the icy lake until
some one came to drive the buck away, and to
witness his humiliation! The blood rushed to
his bronzed and bearded cheeks at the thought,
though he was now shivering to his marrow
with the combined cold of water and wind.

In desperation he suddenly made a great
splashing and waved his arms wildly about his
head, then gave a piercing yell.

This inexplicable behavior of his victim had
its effect on the buck. Irresolutely he fell
back a few steps, startled by the wild commotion; and at the terrifying sound that followed
his ardor for battle died. His madness cool-

Pawing the gravel and shaking his antlers in invitation to combat

ing as suddenly as aroused, with a snort of dismay Scarside whirled in his tracks and dashed off through the trees.

Grim of visage but with chattering teeth Laban climbed out of the water, beached his canoe, and hurried homeward, flailing his great arms against his body to restore the sluggish blood. Half-way home he met Lonny coming over the trail.

"Was that you yelled, Pop? Sounded like some one was terribly hurted, or somethin'— what in time's the matter, anyway! Upset?" Lonny gazed wonderingly at the dripping, angry-faced figure of his father.

"Yes, somethin' 's happened, but ye need n't blat it 'round 'mongst the neighbors. An' somethin' else 's goin' to happen, too, mighty soon!"

As his father related his adventure with Old Scarside, Lonny had difficulty in repressing the chuckles that rose to his lips. He covered his mouth with his hand to hide the grin that would persist.

" 'T aint no laughin' matter," protested

37

Laban, noting the action. "Ef I don't catch pneumony from it I 'll be lucky. Jest as soon 's I c'n git some dry duds on I 'm a-goin' to take the rifle an' trail that blame' critter till I git him. 'T ain't enough fer him to be destroyin' the crops; he 's started to attack folks, an' he 's too dangerous to let live." He clamped his mouth on his resolution; and Lonny knew that the big buck of the Swift-water country was doomed.

The scar-sided buck, resting on a mossy knoll in the depths of the spruce wood, raised his head to a suspicous odor that drifted down the wind. He rose to his feet and ran with the breeze for a short distance, then swung around and headed back, paralleling his trail. He halted in a clump of tangled low growth a few rods from it, and waited. Soon a man came swinging along, silent-footed, carrying that dreaded black stick, his eyes bent on the ground but now and again lifting to scan the surrounding bush. Manifestly, as the evidence of nose and eyes indicated to the buck,

38

this was the same human so lately visited with his displeasure; and some elemental intuition that reprisal was to be expected warned the animal that he must be discreet.

When the man had passed, the buck quietly withdrew from his hiding-place and bounded off at right angles to the trail. A mixture of wariness and confidence guided his actions during the succeeding hours. He well knew the danger of giving the man a glimpse of himself in circumstances like these, but his great craft, so often successfully exercised, and his long immunity from harm, had bred in him a confidence in his powers that stayed his flight to the barest necessity of keeping out of range. Doggedly the hunter followed, untangling the puzzles of the trail so cunningly woven, his skill the fruit of many a previous stalking of the wily old buck. But whereas on these other occasions he had been content to consider himself the victor in the contest of wits, when he finally had come within easy shooting-distance of his quarry, bravely withstanding the itch of his trigger-finger, this time there

GREEN-TIMBER TRAILS

would be a different ending to the hunt.

As the pursuit lengthened, familiar land-marks apprized the backwoodsman that the buck was circling back toward the settlement. This was fortunate, for the afternoon was waning, and furthermore it afforded Laban the opportunity of cutting across to the run-ways along the ridge, where logically the buck would pass. And then, the finish!

The man put his plan into operation. If he hurried he could attain a vantage-point on a rise of ground commanding the flank of the ridge, and here he would have an ideal chance for a shot as the buck swept across the burn-ing that gashed its forested sides. He neared the spot somewhat winded with his exertions, and paused for a moment to regain his breath before carefully threading the thicket of young alder and birch beyond which the earth fell away into the little valley that lay between. Reaching the fringe of the growth, the oppo-site slope was revealed to his sight, and he ex-ulted inwardly as he glimpsed the object of his chase just about to cross the burned area.

THE SWIFTWATER BUCK

The deer was going steadily but at no great speed, and though the shot was a long one, he presented an easy chance for a marksman of Laban's skill.

Without hurry Laban raised the rifle to his shoulder. At the same instant the buck swerved, stood tense for a second, and began to rear and whirl about in a most astonishing manner. Puzzled by this behavior, which made a killing shot uncertain, Laban lowered his rifle to study the meaning of it. He could discern nothing to account for the deer's actions, and when the buck momentarily presented a broadside target, he aimed quickly and pressed the trigger. As he did so there came to him a flash of understanding as the scene suddenly cleared to his eyes, and his brain fought to restrain the pressure of his finger; but too late. The rifle cracked and the buck went down, and Laban rushed over to the hillside, a numbing fear rising in his heart.

The scar-sided buck had begun to be annoyed at the pertinacity of the man who fol-

41

lowed him. All the cunning that so often in the past had served him seemed of no avail against this creature, who solved each mystery of the trail with such seeming ease. But he was not yet fearful; his bag of tricks was still far from empty. Therefore without panic he broke through the trees that bordered the fire-devastated sweep of ground, heading diagonally for the summit, whence, in the shielding second growth that clothed the spine of the ridge, a view of his adversary's progress might be had. Midway in his flight up the acclivity, a terrifying odor suddenly smote his nostrils. He pivoted sharply as the mingled scent of man and a worse-hated enemy warned him of danger close by, and sought warily to locate it.

As his head lifted his gaze fell on a long, tawny, furtive beast crawling serpent-wise through the low brush, its tail twitching at the tip, while at a little distance in front a small man creature lay twisted on the ground, wriggling frantically but not moving from the spot. The eyes of the stricken creature bore on him at the same instant, and a cry came from its lips, cut short as it sagged into an inert heap.

Who shall say what promptings stirred within the whitetail buck, impelling him to leap furiously upon the most dreaded of his animal foes? Whether at the cry he recognized the young human who had grown so engagingly familiar to him, and sensed the appeal in it, or merely in the season of his queer flashes of insane courage his hatred for the slinking beast flamed into uncontrollable rage, no man may say. Howbeit, the big cat, crouching for the spring, and unaware or unmindful of the new-comer upon the scene, was assailed from behind by a fury of fierce-driven blows from feet that cut into his flesh like steel knives. His spine was crushed at the first onslaught, and turning with an agonized snarl he was flattened to the ground by an irresistible array of stabbing bayonet points. So sudden and overwhelming was the attack that the panther had never a chance. Almost before he could realize his plight, the deep-

43

cutting feet and battering antlers had reached his vitals and the spark of his savage life flickered out. But as the victorious buck prodded at the now unresponsive form, a rifle shot shattered the silence, and at the report he gave a convulsive leap forward and fell a-sprawl, his nose lying against the same hand that he had nuzzled confidingly in a long-past day.

As Laban breathlessly drew near, the full meaning of the strange scene was made plain to him. A sharp pang of regret for the slaying of his son's deliverer came to the backwoodsman as he bent over the huddled, unconscious form and saw that the child was not seriously hurt. A foot tightly held in a tangle of roots and twisted at the ankle indicated the nature of Lonny's mishap. Thankful that it was no worse, Laban cut away the mass and gently chafed the boy back to life. In a few minutes Lonny was sitting up, nursing his sprained ankle, the pain of which was almost forgotten in his wonder at what he beheld.

"Old Scarside saved you from the painter, Lonny, an' what he got fer it was a bullet! I'd give the rifle ef I'd sensed what was up a second sooner. I see somethin' o' what was happenin' in a flash, but 'twas too late. I'm mortal sorry I killed the critter."

Lonny sorrowfully patted the sleek, tawny neck that lay stretched at his feet. Tears were not far from his eyes, and not for the pain of his wrenched foot. "The old feller knew it was me—I allus told you he knew me! —an' he wasn't goin' to let me be chawed up by no painter." Never thereafter in the many tellings of the story was either to permit this altruistic motive for the buck's action to be gainsaid.

"How'd you git inter such a mess, I want t' know?" asked his father as the boy thoughtlessly tried to rise to his feet for a closer view of the mangled body of the panther.

Lonny sank back, stifling a yelp of pain. "I come out here to see if I couldn't turn Old Scarside off the ridge if he happened along with you after him," he admitted; "an' I

45

ketched my foot in this here mess o' creepers an' like to broke my ankle when I fell. I could n't move, hardly, an' then that ornery painter came lopin' along an' saw me an' started creepin' up—" he shivered at memory of the sinister, stealthy approach of the big cat, its brassy, malevolent eyes fastened with savage purpose on the shrinking lad whom its cowardly heart knew to be disabled. "I tried to crawl off, but my foot was held tight; an' I just looked at the varmint an' tried to yell, but was too scairt. An' then I saw Old Scarside amblin' out o' the woods like he was comin' to help me an' I called to him— an' that 's all I remember.

"You come, did n't you, old feller?" he addressed his fallen champion. "It 's a blame' shame you got killed fer what you did fer me." The hot tears this time overflowed.

"Wonder where I hit him," said Laban, awkwardly seeking to cover his own very real misery. "Don 't see nary mark, an' there ain't no blood, fer as I kin tell. S'pose I might as well bleed him," he added, practicalities not to be lost sight of even in the face of tragedy. He drew his knife from its sheath and bent over the body, one hand grasping the antlers.

The moment that followed was the most bewildering in the lives of father and son. For an instant they seemed to be inextricably entangled in a maze of wildly threshing limbs —their own and a deer's—as the "dead" buck rose in the air with a terrified snort, sending Laban spread-eagling over upon Lonny, and, finding his feet after a few frantic seconds, sped off into the timber.

Astonishment held the two speechless for a space. Then Lonny, ignoring the throbbing pain of his foot from the shaking up, gave voice to a yell of joy.

"Go it, Scarside! Go it!" he shrieked jubilantly after the vanishing buck. "Could n't kill you after all, you old rip-snorter, could they!" Full vent for his feelings at the deer's startling resurrection demanded nothing less than the turning of several handsprings, but Lonny could only toss his hat in the air and wave his arms exultantly. He turned shining eyes on his father, over whose face a delighted grin was breaking as he rubbed his bruises. "You must 've jest creased him, Pa, an' only knocked him out fer a spell. Gosh, but I 'm glad!"

"You bet I 'm glad, too!" chuckled Laban, "even ef 't was the second time to-day the critter sent me sprawlin'. Reckon when I pulled the trigger an' then tried not to, all to once, I must 've lost my bead an' shot high. Likely the ball nicked him at the base o' the antlers an' the shock keeled him over, but did n't hurt him none. 'T was a rank miss that I 'm proud of—an' 't will be the last time any one from hereabouts takes a shot at the old buck, I promise ye that!

"Well, I reckon we better be gittin' home; I 'll carry ye pickaback." He swung the lad up to his broad shoulders and started along the back trail for the clearing.

As the big backwoodsman strode homeward through the lengthening woodland shadows, his chattering, light-hearted burden clinging

48

to his neck, he marveled thankfully at the outcome of the day's adventures and framed the
edict he would send forth upon the morrow,
to be violated only at peril of Laban Knowles's
vengeance.

The scar-sided buck, plunging through the
twilight aisles of the spruce wood, could not
know that from this day he would have nothing to fear from his human neighbors of the
wilderness border. Nor that before many
hours the story of his exploit would go ring-
ing through the settlements, colored into a
supreme act of devotion to his youthful patron,
and given an imperishable page in the annals
of the Swiftwater country.

THE MADCAPS OF THE WATERS

THE MADCAPS OF THE WATERS

WITH the coming of twilight a shroud of brooding quiet spread over the wild, rock-grit Northern lake, around whose shadowy rim a vestige of ice still clung. The early spring winds, not yet bereft of their winter chill, were dying gustily with the sun's setting, while the furtive day-prowling life of the marge, huddled snugly in its coverts, drowsed into the long night's sleep. Before the mantling dusk had quenched the crimson and orange flames of the Western horizon, two tiny black specks rose into the cloudless vault above the ragged crest of the fir forest that skirted the lake's Southern border. Swiftly the specks enlarged until the sturdy wings that bore them quivered against the dimming blue background. Faintly at first, then in a swelling crescendo, the wild, weird notes of a clarion cry filled the heavens with eery music. In undulating volume, as the winds of the upper levels willed, the eldritch sound floated earthward, stirring the inhabitants of the woodland glooms to sleepy protest. But it brought only a passing tremor to their hearts; the wildings knew it for the herald song of the loons, spring migrants from the Southland returning to their Northern home for the nesting.

When the travellers were just above the lower boundary of the lake the clamor hushed abruptly as they dipped in their flight; and swerving down a by-path of the windy aerial roadways, the swift-winging birds headed in a long slant toward the water. Like feathered black stones from a catapult the great gooselike bodies struck the lake's placid bosom, ploughing over it in an upflung smother of spray until the impetus of their long, swift flight was spent. Then with noisily flapping wings and necks outstretched they rose upon the surface until they seemed to stand upright on their short, stiff tail-feathers, and from each extended throat issued peal upon peal of wild, exultant laughter. In wanton glee, for a space of minutes the pair crazily dived and

54

swam about in circles, sending the water in silvery cascades over their dark thick-feathered backs, the uncanny merriment of their voices multiplied into a demoniac medley by the rocky walls of the lake.

Suddenly, as by a signal, the mad frolic ceased, and turning toward the shore the loons swam sedately into a little remembered cove, and in a tangle of last year's matted growth just beyond the water's edge composed themselves for the night.

Thus the mated pair of great Northern divers returned to their summer home in the far upper country, here to build their nests and rear their young as they had in previous years. Self-appointed guardians of the lake's surface —and tyrants of its deeps—the loons held sway disputed only by the turtles and muskrats and mink and an occasional otter; for the pebbly bottom failed to sprout the wild rice, so that the ducks seldom gave it more than a passing glance, and the lordly, high-winging geese would not deign to harbor in its narrow confines.

After a day of rioting among the teeming finny life of the depths, to satisfy the keen edge of their winter's hunger for the firm, sweet flesh of Northern trout, the pair set about their nest-building. At the upper end of the lake a spit of weedy, boggy soil running out into shoal water was selected; and at the extreme tip of this the loons scraped together a heap of dried rush-stems and moss and little sticks, and trod and brushed it into the semblance of a nest. Here the two brown-olive, umber-spotted eggs were laid, where the brooding female could sweep the adjacent levels with eyes ever alert for four-footed marauders and quest the upper spaces for winged enemies.

At times the male bird, differing from his mate only in being a trifle larger, kept her company, but more often he occupied his days in exploring the lake and pursuing the toothsome trout and lesser fry wherewith to appease his voracious appetite. For a short while each day the female joined him in his aquatic forays, to secure for herself a meal of fish. On these occasions she left her nest with so

little betraying motion that she seemed merely
to tip over the edge of it and disappear in the
ripples.   Swimming below, she rose beside her
mate at some distance from the nest, and at
once began a mad scramble atop and beneath
the surface to limber up her stiffened muscles.
For a space they chased each other about like
wild things suddenly gone stark mad, then
suddenly loosed a long, quavering cry upon
the silences and betook themselves to the depths
in quest of food, twin marvels of grace and
speed and proficiency in their pursuit of the
under-water inhabitants.   Turning, doubling,
twisting, as inexorably as fate they followed
the wildly darting fish, until one or the other,
seizing a victim in a viselike bill, rose to the
surface.   With a sidewise jerk of the head
the captor would toss the fish into the air,
catch it as it fell head-first, and gulp it down
in a trice, and with lungs replenished dive
again to seek further spoils.   With her hunger
satisfied the female returned to her eggs by
the same submerged route, again to brood
away the long hours while the sun grew gradu-

ally warmer and the lush grasses slowly wove a concealing screen about the nesting-place.

In June the chicks were hatched. Two awkward little balls of slate-colored down, they tumbled about grotesquely on land, but displayed the inherited grace of their parents when in the water. Here in the shallows where the shade of the alders screened them effectually from prying eyes the tiny pair passed their schooling in the art of swimming and diving. And before they were many days old the baby loons were practising on the shiners and chubs and minnows that tenanted the shoals; and very adept they became in the matter of out-swimming their small, slippery victims. As they grew older the parent birds left them alone for short periods while they went to fish farther out in the depths, doubtless with many cautionings as to their conduct in keeping within the shadows of the bank and avoiding the ambush of enemies in the thick-growing sedges.

One day, while the parents were half the lake's width from the fledglings, an outcry of startled, distressed pipings reached their hearing. In an instant the two started in splashing haste toward the sound. Half flying, half running over the surface, wings and feet beating the water into foam in their scramble to ascertain what trouble the youngsters were in, they rapidly drew near the scene. Then, seeming to grasp the situation, they disappeared in a smooth dive.

Over near the bank the young loons had been disporting themselves in infantile enjoyment of the balmy early summer morning. Their cheepings and pipings were low-toned and discreet, and danger seemed not to exist in their pleasant watery world. Suddenly one of them, venturing out near the edge of the shallows where the bottom shelved abruptly, was seized by the leg by some unseen terror and drawn toward the deeps. Strong and lusty by this time, when he found himself unwillingly immersed in the element wherein he had learned to be thoroughly at home, he fought with all his acquired knowledge of the use of wings and feet to regain the surface. True, one foot was held fast in a cruel grip, but the other worked fast and furious and his half-feathered wings beat valiantly against the down-pull. Flying in the water rather than swimming is the loon's method, and the strong thrust of his wings overcame for a moment the effort of the big turtle that had hold of him. The terrified youngling finally was able to win upward into the air, though only for a brief moment could he possibly overcome that inexorable weight that dragged savagely at his foot. In the instant that he emerged his tiny voice sent plaintive, terror-stricken appeals across the lake, while his wings threshed the water in an agonized effort to release himself from the clutch. His sister, paddling distractedly around the spot where he had disappeared in so unusual a manner, fearful for this once of diving down where assuredly there lurked some awful, unknown horror, joined her voice with his as he came up, and instantly the medley of heartrending calls brought a strident answer from afar as the larger birds hastened to the rescue.

Slowly the turtle was sinking with its prize toward the weedy
bottom

Hardly had the unfortunate chick filled his lungs with air when he was pulled below again, his struggles weakening with the strain on his tender muscles. Slowly the turtle was sinking with its prize toward the weedy bottom where he could devour the morsel unmolested, when of a sudden the tough sinews of his outstretched neck were pierced and torn apart by a daggerlike weapon as the mother loon drove her bill unerringly and with tremendous strength through the assassin's one vulnerable spot. Often in the past had the loons clashed their stout sword points impotently against the turtles' armor, while the reptiles with heads and feet withdrawn into impregnable shells sulked safely within their protecting walls until the danger had passed. But this time the greed of the hungry marauder was his undoing, and the air from his punctured throat bubbled upward as he received the death thrust.

Luckily for the young loon the mother's bill had slanted up into the turtle's tightly-locked jaw muscles, which were sheared through as by a knife. The ugly mandibles opened, freeing the captive, and like a dart he shot to the surface. Jerking her bill with no little difficulty from the stringy flesh, the mother watched for an instant the frantic assaults of her mate upon the slowly sinking shell, then rose and swam round and round her rescued offspring in comforting solicitude; while the male, coming up after pursuing his dying enemy to the bottom, splashed about in rageful excitement. The lacerated leg of the young loon bothered him in his diving and swimming for a few days, then healed and was forgotten.

About this time, when the days were growing hot with the full power of the summer sun, the male bird felt coming upon him the old midyear impulse to flee from family cares for a period. The season of the moult had arrived, and it behooved him to absent himself so that both he and his mate might, as custom willed, change their feathered garments in seclusion from each other. Wherefore one day he breasted a vagrant wind that puffed its ruffling path across the lake, and rising into it with heavy awkwardness, soon caught his wing stroke and mounted in a swift incline to the upper air. No message of farewell marked his going. Straight for a remembered lake a few miles to the north he headed, and at the end of his flight dropped upon the surface of a lonely stretch of water with a wandering, irregular shore line lying within a range of low hills. Here he disported himself and fed upon the rich fare of the depths, in carefree bachelordom, while the transformation of his feathers slowly took place.

One day as he was cruising lazily about on the sunflecked water, with sharp, bright eyes peering inquisitively this way and that from the graceful head that now was taking on a new iridescence in the warm glow, his sight fell upon something that was strangely alien to this secluded domain. But the intruder was not wholly unfamiliar to one of the loon's widely traveled habit. He knew from experience the nature of this floating object that sought so clumsily by human guidance to emulate his own graceful progress on the lake's

GREEN-TIMBER TRAILS

expanse; and here at last, he realized, was one
of those unwelcome man creatures come to disturb his tranquillity and violate the calm of
his own water world and the dusky green
silences that encompassed it.

Perturbed though he was by the apparition,
his habitual curiosity was none the less upper-
most in him, and he bore down upon the birch-
bark and its occupant in a questioning mood.
The man was engaged in some peculiar opera-
tions that seemingly had to do with the under-
water denizens, for ever and again he drew in
and paid out long, slender lines that occasionally brought a glittering, writhing fish over the
side of his craft. Cautiously the loon drew
nearer to the disquieting though fascinating
spectacle; but he could not hope to remain for
long unseen by the busy fisherman. His new
feathering had transformed the slaty black of
his upper body into a striking white-checkered
pattern, and his creamy cravat and the white-
spangled necklace encircling his throat, above
which glistened a head of burnished green and
blue metallic hues, all contrasted vividly with

64

the pellucid gray of the water and its emerald shores.

At a quick lift of the man's head the loon's body lowered cannily in the water without apparent volition, until only his long-billed head showed above the surface. But he had been seen, as he was well aware. The man snatched something from the bottom of his craft and a spurt of flame issued from the weapon held to his shoulder, followed by a hail of pellets upon the surface where the bird had rested. But the loon already had sunk his body, and before the charge arrived had dived at the flash and was speeding through the depths. At a distant point he emerged, and his shrill, defiant notes rang out tantalizingly as the man shifted his aim and the weapon spoke again. But once more came the lightning-swift dive at the flash, followed by a harmless spattering of shot in the swirl that marked his disappearance.

Again and again the comedy was enacted, the scene shifting gradually toward the center of the lake, as the man with an occasional hurried stroke of his paddle sent the canoe out into the open water. But the wily bird had now a double advantage, and, turning as he dived, darted beneath his enemy, whose ears suddenly were assailed from behind by a peal of mocking laughter, as the loon emerged in the wake of his pursuer's craft. Always he rose where least expected by the now thoroughly exasperated fisherman, sometimes afar and sometimes so perilously near to the death-spouting weapon that his derisive cry was cut short by the quick necessity of diving in the hair's breadth of time that intervened between flash and leaden hail. And always he sent forth his plaintive, jeering call as he came up, and always his marvelous quickness enabled him to escape the deadly messengers that answered his challenge. Until at length, patience and ammunition alike exhausted, the human whom he had set at defiance gave up the contest and swept back to the lower margin and faded from view around a bend. Rising on the surface to his full height, at his adversary's acceptance of defeat, the loon voiced his derision exultantly in a long-drawn, hollow cry, then turned and sped over the darkening water away from the scene of his triumph.

In the days that followed, the loon continued his observation of the intruder's activities and evaded the various stratagems that were employed by the man to shoot or capture him. The desire to return to his family was growing within him, for he had by now acquired his complete change of plumage and the time for his departure was at hand; but overweening curiosity—or was it defiance?—held him to the lake.

One late afternoon of a day when his keen vision had failed to spy the object of his interest in any of the coves where usually he was to be found, the loon was engaging in his favorite pastime of fishing. Chubs and minnows and redfins had proved plentiful and easy of capture, but he was still unsatisfied. Deep down among the filmy, translucent shadows of the bottom growth he quested more toothsome and gamier quarry, weaving in and out among the stems and fronds of this miniature forest in a swift zigzag course, his quick-seeing eyes alert for the crimson-speckled aristocrat of the waters which his appetite craved. Suddenly he glimpsed an unsuspecting trout apparently engaged in gorging its own dinner of a silver-sided minnow. With the full power of wings and feet he hurled himself toward the spotted beauty, neck and head outstretched, tipped by the rapier point of his hard black bill.

The trout saw him coming, but instead of flashing away through the network of weeds, darted about within a small radius, his progress impeded in some strange manner. To seize the terror-stricken victim was absurdly simple. Never before had the loon known so short-lived a chase of the lake's choicest provender. But, to his bewilderment, as his wide-opened bill closed upon the fish he was conscious of a stabbing pang at the base of his upper mandible, a piercing of the roof of his mouth such as the slight finspines of a trout assuredly could not cause. The pain and puzzle of this startled him into releasing his captive; but the trout still seemed to cling about his beak, and the sharp, stinging barb would not be dislodged.   In a panic he turned to flee from the spot, but was brought up suddenly by a check that nearly jerked his neck out of joint. His lungs by this time were aching for air, and he forced himself upward to replenish them. He succeeded in reaching the surface in spite of the pull, and once there fought with splashing energy to free himself of the horror that bit so savagely into the horny layers of his mouth; but struggle as he might he could not escape the torment, though he had managed to shake off the bothersome trout.   And in a few moments his fear and wrath were further inflamed by the sight of his human opponent paddling toward the spot where he was churning the water into foam in his wild striving for freedom.

"Got ye now!" the loon heard the hated man-voice exclaim.   "Reckon I 'll have that there cap o' loon feathers I sot my mind on, after all," exulted his enemy.   "Did n't look fer to ketch ye on my set-lines, but ye 'll make a right good haul, jest the same." Dropping his paddle while yet some distance from the disturbance, the man reached over the side and seized an end of the heavy cord to which the dangling baited lines were attached and began pulling it into the canoe, hand over hand.

At the spoken words the loon, in a fury of hate and dread, dived to the limit of the line. With all the vigor of his webbed feet and sturdy wings he sought to stay the merciless drag or to snap that slender bond that was so unbelievably tenacious. But his endeavors would not avail, though his strength and courage enabled him to retard the man's efforts appreciably. At length his bursting lungs could no longer stand the strain of his long submersion and with the urgent need for air he thrust violently for the surface.

The trot-line had bellied outward and the tough, pliant stake to which the farther end was attached had bent against his frenzied tugging, so that the return pull when the tension was relaxed drew the loon from his upward path. And to this impulse was added the rapid hauling in of the line by the gloating poacher. Deflected in his course, and with speed thus augmented, the half-blinded bird shot obliquely through the water with the rush of a projectile straight toward the bobbing craft.

Head on, the loon smashed into the canoe, his bill striking the upper edge just where the man grasped it with one hand to steady himself against the sudden giving of the line. His iron beak nearly severed the gripping fingers as it ploughed a furrow across the man's knuckles; and with the impact against the cedar gunwale the hook was broken out of its hold with an excruciating wrench. The yell of pain and astonishment that smote his hearing quickened the loon's momentarily dazed senses and he dived, but hardly in advance of the man who, unbalanced by the shock, was neatly toppled overboard by the cranky birch-bark.

Out of the commotion swam the loon at his swiftest, to escape the vengeful being who assuredly intended to pursue him in his own element. He kept below until his overtaxed lungs

71

demanded air, shooting up for a hurried gulp and then down again and onward until once more he was forced to rise for breath. This time he rose high out of the water to scan his surroundings. It was evident that he had not been followed, after all. Back there near the shore was his persecutor, floundering in the mud and weeds of the shallows to gain the bank. Through the gathering dusk the loon saw him scramble out on dry land and stand shaking his fist over the lake. But his keen hearing detected only the angry note in the torrent of human sounds that floated across to him, as the man shouted maledictions on the rival fisherman who had so nearly caused his drowning.

Joying in his freedom, the loon suddenly felt a great loneliness, and there came irresistibly to him the call of his kind. The belated inclination to rejoin his family swept into his wild heart, and launching himself on the breeze he mounted to the heights. There he set his course, and swiftly winging down the paths of air, homeward bound, back to the deserted lake and his discomfited enemy he sent his melancholy scornful farewell.

"Wu-loo, wu-loo-loo, wu-loo-oo-o!" echoed his song from aloft, the oft-repeated cry filling the heavens with mournful cadence as the fast-journeying bird neared the home waters where his mate and her half-grown brood awaited his return.

73

IN WILD-STRAWBERRY TIME

IN WILD-STRAWBERRY TIME

THE early morning light washed in a gray wave over the dark-green crest of the spruce forest, and shortly the intervale was suffused with shimmering gold as the sun's first beams fell upon the mist curtain that overhung the low-lying ground. Each tiny atom of moisture among the millions in the dew-laden atmosphere reflected the golden tint radiantly, then slowly dimmed and was absorbed by the new warmth that came creeping into the air. As the last curling wisps of vapor dissolved, the sunlight swept over the wild meadow, disclosing its rich enameling of wild flowers and lush green grass. Where the earth dipped slightly to hold the seeping water of a turbulent stream that flowed near by, a shallow mere fringed with purple-glowing flag was the last to yield its dew coverlet to the spreading rays.

Emerging from the black wall of trees that rimmed this quiet glade, a she bear with a single cub at her side cast appraising eyes over the sparkling expanse. Halting for a moment at the meadow's edge, she sniffed the air inquiringly, then shambled through the wet grass to drink at the pool. The cub's tiny bright eyes snapped with mischievous interest in each object that met his view. He suppressed his exuberance, however, for already he knew that quietness and caution were advisable in the open spaces until they were examined thoroughly for possible lurking dangers.

The mother bear drank of the clear, cool water, and with her morning thirst satisfied quested the meadow for breakfast. The cub was in the kindergarten stage of schooling and learning to supplement the lessening maternal supply of nourishment with more solid food. With twinkling baby eyes he watched his mother as she sought the roots of Indian turnip and prairie crocus and ploughed them up with her snout. The cub sampled them and found the crocus roots eatable, but the pungency of the Indian turnip was rather too biting for his sensitive throat. Anyway, he had breakfasted on more familiar food back in the warm den under an overhanging rock in the heart of the forest, and was not very hungry; and after gratifying a merely curious interest in the provender which his mother found so appetizing, he nuzzled her furry black flank impatiently.

When the roots palled she accepted the hint and the two moved off toward the stream. Here the old bear sniffed along the water's edge, seeking any disabled fish that might have been cast up, and rooted among the stones in the shallows for tadpoles. A scurrying crawfish she hooked up with her claws and drew to the bank for her offspring's edification, watching him with shrewd eyes as he cautiously moved it about with his paw and smelt the strange-appearing thing suspiciously. A nip on his tender muzzle from the tiny pincers sent him back on his haunches with a whimper of astonishment; and the mother, apparently satisfied with this first lesson in the habits of crawfish, crushed it beneath her foot and swallowed the titbit with smacking satisfaction.

The stream yielded very little food this morning and her hearty appetite impelled her to seek a more bountiful repast. Giving the cub a low, guttural command to follow, she started off across the meadow and into the woods, heading for a chain of burnt hills that lay to the east. On the other side of this low range she knew of certain unused pasturelands where grew a fruit much to her liking.

A part of the way was rough going, and she frequently helped the cub along over the boulder-strewn rise of ground, pushing him up with her nose and occasionally cuffing him into action when he hesitated before the obstacles that lay in their path. At length they passed over the crest of the rise, bald of trees save for the somber gray rampikes that thrust upward out of the undergrowth—stark ghosts of hardwood killed by a forest fire that had swept the ridge many years before. They threaded their way through these grim sentinel boles and scrambled down the slope to gain the open ground that lay below. This was a stretch of stump-land pasture where a settler once had grazed his meager flocks, but long deserted and now with little likelihood of human intrusion.

As the two descended to the open an enticing fragrance in the air caused the older bear to sniff hungrily and shuffle along at a faster gait. The pleasing aromatic quality that reached her nose arose from a low dense growth that matted the ground—a carpet of wild strawberries, the tiny deep-red fruit glowing brilliantly among the half-shielding green leaves. Here the rich humus of the ancient forest floor in which they were rooted fed the berries lavishly; and watered by the limpid night dews they developed an ambrosial perfection of flavor quite unknown in the cultivated variety. The early summer sun had ripened them and set the sugar in their delicate tissues, and their delectable profusion promised rich feasting.

The older bear fell to the feast ravenously. She curled her long, thin red tongue around each heavily clustered plant and drew fruit and leaves into her mouth, expelling the coarser leaves and stalks and champing the luscious berries noisily. As she gulped them down she expressed her relish of their spicy sweetness with low grunts and woofs.

The cub watched her with interested eyes. Here was something in the way of food that was new to him, and apparently it was a very desirable food. The mother occasionally ceased her feeding to nudge him while she rumbled low in her throat, evidently to encourage the youngster to emulate her methods. His sharp little teeth pierced the delicate pulp and he licked the sweet juice from his lips and found it distinctly pleasing. The forest younglings learn rapidly, and soon he was eating with greedy delight. At first he seized the berries with his teeth, but he quickly found the proper use of his tongue in gathering the clusters.

He ate until he could hold no more, his skin stretched so tight with his first meal of strawberries that he could scarcely waddle along

She licked the sticky sweetness from his soft fur

after his more capacious mother. Finally even her enormous appetite was glutted, and she sought a warm grassy pocket between the roots of a large stump and curled up to bask in the grateful midday heat while she digested her cloying meal. The cub sprawled beside her, his little paunch ludicrously distended. She licked the sticky sweetness of the feast from his soft fur while he alternately dozed and made protesting passes with his paws at the solicitous maternal face.

When he had rested long enough to feel the need of renewed activity, his playful sallies ended his mother's sleepy comfort, and she rose and sauntered off across the pasture, the cub following in her footsteps. She knew this region of old and was aware that the small group of primitive farm buildings that lay at the pasture's lower edge had been forsaken by their former human occupants. She had all a bear's overweening curiosity and felt to-day in a mood to gratify it concerning these peculiar dens that once had harbored the enemy of her kind. Until the present she had

not succeded in getting her courage up to the
point of investigating the log structures, but
now she sensed in their long-continued deso-
lation a promise of safety, and she approached
them without misgivings.

No trace of human odor lay around the little
abandoned farmstead. She nosed about the
cabin and crude pole sheds expectant of discovering something of an eatable nature; but nothing rewarded her keen nostrils save the medley
of scents left by porcupines and mice and squirrels that for years had made the place a
rendezvous. From his perch on the ridge-pole
of the cabin, a red squirrel discovered her
presence, and ran up and down the moss-
grown "scoop" roof, chattering wrathful in-
sults at the intruders. The bear eyed him
maliciously for a moment, then ignored the insolent little blackguard and continued her explorations.

The cub at first kept close to his mother's
side, ill at ease in these strange surroundings.
But gradually youthful curiosity overcame his

timidity and he strayed from the protecting presence to do a little investigating on his own account. While he sought to fathom the mystery of some rotting timbers overgrown with weeds that lay in the rear of the cabin, the old bear pursued her vague quest around the outbuildings.

A sudden muffled squalling brought her racing toward the sound, fur bristling along her back and eyes snapping with angry apprehension. The cry was plainly for help, and she was ready to battle any living thing that threatened her offspring. But no marauder was in sight, nor even the cub, for that matter, though the plaintive squeals still filled the air, sounding strangely unreal but unmistakably his and quite near to her. Puzzled and anxious, she sought out his tracks with her nose, but these were so crisscrossed that they only confused her. Her rangings gradually drew the distracted mother closer to the outcry, and at last she knew that it arose from the clump of weeds. Picking her way over the crumbling wood at their roots she came upon a yawning black hole whence the pitiful summons issued.

The cub had tumbled into an old well, the wooden curb of which lay in decay about its mouth, overgrown with a screening mass of green. Fortunately it was dry and so matted at the bottom with litter that the force of his fall was broken, and the fat little body had suffered nothing worse than a severe shaking up. Terror-stricken with the sudden plunge and the quick enveloping blackness, he squawled miserably for his mother.

Soon he heard her questioning calls and saw the silhouette of her head against the disk of blue light above him. But her arrival brought only the comfort of her presence; she was incapable of rescuing him.

With yearning eyes the mother bear circled the opening, crouching at the brink now and again to look down into the dark hole, whining anxiously and with low rumblings bidding him to try to climb up. The cub whimpered in reply, and strove vainly to find footing up the straight walls. At first she could not discern the small black-furred form in the denser blackness of the bottom, but as her ceaseless trampling about the edge broke down the weeds the light filtered in and made it possible for her to distinguish him. She flattened herself on the ground beside the well and stretched down first one fore-paw and then the other in a fruitless attempt to reach the imploring little captive; and once she tentatively backed to the verge to essay a descent by the usual bear method. But the crumbling of the earth as she sought for a foothold with her hind-feet discouraged her, and she renewed her circling and impotent whining entreaties.

Suddenly she lifted her head to a new and startling sound. It was the beat of quick footfalls that came to her ears, and as they drew closer she growled menacingly and bared her teeth in sullen defiance. Whatever it might be, it was advancing upon the cabin from the pasture, and dimly she associated the intruder with her cub's imprisonment in the pitfall. This of a certainty was the author of his mishap, and all her dormant ferocity blazed into being as she lurched forward to give battle to the unknown enemy before it could complete its designs. It was coming rapidly nearer and she rushed to the front of the cabin to intercept it. As the enraged mother bear rounded the building a flying form darted inside before she could strike it down, and the door crashed shut against her snarling, savagely grinning face.

And to her angry amazement the following instant she was assailed from behind by a screeching fury of teeth and claws. Immediately she found herself engaged in a battle to the death with a second enemy of whose approach she had received no warning.

A little earlier this same day an ancient buckboard holding two young people deeply interested in each other crept over a seldom-traveled backwoods road that skirted the eastern edge of the abandoned farm. The slender, pretty girl seated beside the sturdy youth who was driving looked up into his eyes shyly as he told her of his plans for the future. Happily the plough-horse drawing the ramshackle vehicle was set and staid in his ways; else the young country swain could not have given so much of his gaze to the fresh, blue-eyed face upturned to his own.

Jeff had jumped at the hint dropped by the girl's mother that Sally was to return home that day from her spell of nursing old Mis' Hammersmith at Big Forks; and he had volunteered to go and fetch her. Big Jeff Tucker for many months had held certain well-defined ideas on an aspect of these large plans of his which he had not yet come to in his telling of them. But perhaps Sally Ingalls was not so unaware of what they might be as he imagined. Jeff's eyes said much that his tongue found it difficult to frame. Now he was leading up to the most important phase of his dreams, for the opportunity he had long sought had come; and the time and place were an inspiration for the avowal.

An unclouded summer sun distilled from

the red-fruited chokecherry thickets and massed blooms of brier rose and wild raspberry lining the rutted tracks an essence that the light breezes dissolved into an unmatchable fragrance. And young blood was responding to the urge of the perfumed air, vibrant with the cheerful notes of song-sparrows and the carols of flashing thistle-birds that lighted on swaying milkweed stalks and rose and lighted again farther on as the buckboard with its absorbed occupants pursued them slowly along the winding road.

But the ancient vehicle was traitor to the lover's cause. As it rolled over a "thank-you-marm" on the down grade of a hill the forward axle snapped and broke—and so did the thread of the young man's discourse. At the sudden lurch Jeff threw his arm around Sally's waist to prevent her falling forward upon the horse, who stopped in his tracks as the whiffle-tree came down about his heels. Sally's always blushing cheeks blushed redder with the contact, and she nimbly drew out of his embrace and stepped to the ground. Jeff covered his lapse with a hasty examination of the wrecked vehicle and a string of mild expletives over the mishap.

"Durn the blame' thing! We can't noways get home in it now, Sally," he complained. "Wish I could fasten up that axle, but I hain't got no wire." He pondered over the situation for a moment. "Tell you what we 'll have to do, Sally," he continued. "I 'll tie Whitey here to the fence an' foot it back to the Forks an' get some bale wire; an' you can set here an' wait fer me; I won't be gone more 'n an hour."

"I reckon that 's the best we can do," Sally agreed. "But tell you what, Jeff; 'stead o' waitin' here I 'll tramp over to the old deserted farm an' gather a mess o' wild strawberries. It 's only just across the rise yonder. There 's a sight o' them growin' in the pasture lot an' nobody hardly ever goes there berryin'. You can stop to home with Ma an' me fer supper an' have some o' them, too," she offered, smiling rosily.

Jeff grinned happily. "Now that 's fine,

Sally; you bet I will! An' I got an old grain-bag under the seat you can pick 'em in." He fished it out, and, handing it to Sally, strode rapidly back along the road they had traveled.

Sally's lithe young figure swung easily over the rocky tree-grown rise and shortly she came to the desolate stump-land pasture where the wild strawberries grew. Here the profusion of small scarlet fruit that peeped enticingly from its leafy screen delighted her eyes, and she stood for a moment gazing over the inviting prospect. At the far side of the pasture she had a fleeting glimpse of two bears, mother and cub, just before they vanished around a hummock. The wind was blowing toward Sally and they apparently had not become aware of her presence. The sight brought no fear to the backwoods-bred girl, for she knew that unless provoked into defense the black bears of the region would avoid humankind whenever possible. Rather, she found delight in the incident.

"The cunning thing!" Sally murmured smilingly, as she noted the funny waddling gait of the cub. "He's got a tummy full o' berries, I reckon, an' can only just toddle after his ma."

She fell to picking the fragrant fruit. Gradually she approached the north edge of the pasture, where the gloomy spruce forest reared its dark green-and-black wall. A peculiar chill grew upon her as she drew nearer to the wood. She frowned impatiently at the unpleasant sensation and sought to shrug it away. But it persisted and something impelled her to glance half apprehensively toward the uprearing tree growth.

Her eyes widened with fear at what they beheld, and she knew that she should have heeded earlier the strange warning semiconsciousness of being spied upon by a malignant presence. For a slender, sinuous form, slaty-blue in the shadowy half light of the trees, was gliding toward her. It was a panther, and she shuddered with sickening dread as all the tales she had heard of the animal's cruelty, when once it was inspired to attack a human, flitted through her mind. While her thoughts raced the panther was slowly creeping nearer, its gaunt body hugging the ground, the long tail twitching its premonition of a leap. She still stood staring at it, fascinated by the green-glowing eyes that stared malevolently in return. She knew what the twitching of its tail meant—that the big cat was about to leap forward and in two or three quick, short bounds would be upon her. For an instant she sought to use the power of her eyes to quell its spirit, but the fabled control of wild beasts by this means seemed not to work. With a sharp scream she turned and fled down the gentle slope of the pasture.

Instinctively she headed for the old deserted cabin, the idea that she might possibly gain it and shut herself in against the panther quickly occurring to her. For a brief moment the animal hesitated; the shrill cry dismayed it and it shrank back, snarling in angry fear at the sound of the hated human voice. Its impending spring checked, the girl was given a start that was doubtless the margin between life and death. Then the strong urge that already had overcome its hereditary indisposition to attack a human prevailed again, and encouraged by the girl's evident fright it bounded after her. Its sinewy, graceful body curved over the ground in swift pursuit, but Sally's strong young limbs were fleet and she flew over the springy ground like a deer. For a distance she maintained her lead, but soon she realized with horror that the panther was gaining on her.

As she drew closer to the cabin Sally noted thankfully that the door was open, swung inward, and hope arose within her. With this she gave a spurt and reached the weed-grown dooryard a rod or two in advance of her pursuer.

But just as she was about to plunge through the doorway she was appalled by the sudden apparition that rounded the corner of the cabin. A big black demon of a bear, with surprising agility for so lumbering a body, shot toward her with a ferocious, menacing cough. She saw its gleaming savage teeth and evilly snapping red-rimmed eyes as the

95

beast, almost upon her, struck out savagely with its deadly claw-armed forefoot. But the spurt carried her through the opening a fraction of a second in advance of the blow, and she whirled about and slammed shut the door as the monster's weight was thrown upon it. Pressing her body against the heavy split-planks, she felt feverishly for the fastening, a sudden fear in her heart that there might be none. But her fingers fell upon the rude wooden bar which by good fortune remained intact, and she dropped it quickly into place. Then she sank to the floor, quivering and shaken with the terrible experience.

Almost instantly there arose on the other side of the door a raucous confusion of snarls and growls and thrashing bodies. Sally understood what had taken place; she had not had time to realize the likelihood of this meeting of the two pursuers, and the evidence that her assailants had come together in battle sent her into a spasm of hysterical laughter.

Outside the combat raged fiercely. Seldom does a panther venture to attack a bear, and if the bear has a cub the big cat will avoid a meeting with all possible haste. And the bear, unless it is a she bear whose cub is threatened, will evade conflict with a panther if evasion is comportable with her dignity. The bear is the superior of the two in a fair contest, and is aware of it, but like most of the forest wildings much prefers a truce with its neighbors of nearly equal prowess.

But in this instance the paths of both animals had converged to a common point; each was intent solely on striking down the human who had escaped at the place of meeting and each was inflamed with the lust to kill. As in the bear's cub lay the impelling motive of her attempt to destroy the supposed enemy, so was the panther's own offspring the moving cause of her murderous venture. Fearful of humans as she was, the short commons on which she had subsisted since the recent disappearance of her mate had made her ravenous for food. The drain upon her body by the two always hungry cubs required hearty fare for herself, and if she was to satisfy them she must forage more successfully than she had of late. Consequently when the human who she instinctively knew was the less dangerous of the hated man kind appeared before her eyes as she noiselessly prowled the thickets for game, the pangs of famine overcame her dread. Forthwith she began a furtive stalking of the unsuspecting berry-picker. Had the girl's eyes not been drawn intuitively to the stealthily approaching terror, the hunger-maddened animal would have sprung upon her unawares. But she had heeded the warning of her senses in time, and the flame of the panther's savagery was fanned higher by the balking of its purpose.

When the expected quarry darted into the log sanctuary, and the bear miraculously shot into view at the same instant, the panther had neither opportunity nor inclination to draw back. The bear was interfering with her hunt, the unforgivable breach of law among the wild earthlings, and she descended upon the hulking black interloper in a frenzy of rage and disappointment. The bear was taken at a disadvantage, but turned valiantly to annihilate this insolent disturber of her vengeance. The assailant had secured a firm hold on her back, four sets of sharp hooked claws clinging tenaciously and sinking into her hide, while its punishing fangs sought the channels of life in her neck.

The bear twisted about impotently, then rolled over, the better to dislodge the clutching horror. Her heavy weight nearly crushed the breath out of her enemy's body, but the panther managed to retain her advantage by squirming around until the two were locked in a death grapple face to face. Here the panther was better placed for the deadly work of her claws, and she raked the bear's vulnerable spots with long, eviscerating strokes. The bear was by no means idle with her own deep-cutting weapons, which tore mercilessly at the tawny hide; while both infuriated fighters were employing their savage jaws with ruthless energy.

The bear, being at a woeful disadvantage, was the first to weaken. Her opponent suddenly bored into the relaxing neck and with searching teeth speedily brought an end to the heavier animal's resistance. The bear collapsed in a sprawling, inert black heap, and the victorious cat staggeringly withdrew from her vanquished enemy. The object of her chase forgotten, she dragged her lacerated body away from the battle-ground, and slowly and painfully crawled in the direction of the den where the two hungry cubs awaited her return. The same wild mother-love that had been the underlying cause of the tragedy alone sustained her; but the desperate effort was doomed to fail before she could even reach the shelter of the burnt hills.

Her heart beating wildly as her ferocious jailers fought just outside the door of her refuge, Sally glanced about the cabin for something that she might employ as a weapon in case of need. But nothing offered. She wondered if the victor would try to force an entrance, and how soon the fight would end. One or the other of the animals must soon succumb in the grim contest, the sounds of which betrayed the implacable fury with which they fought. The door looked none too secure, for the hinges were weakened by age and the bar might not withstand a determined onslaught; and there was the open window through which the panther could enter if so disposed. If Jeff were only there! But Jeff could not possibly learn of her predicament; doubtless he was even now waiting at the road for her return, and perhaps was growing uneasy over her absence.

Several times the struggling animals brought up against the door, which creaked ominously with the impact; and once Sally's heart came up into her throat as a particularly violent crash caused several of the decaying wooden pegs of the fastenings to snap under the stress. She leaned her weight against the bulging planks and held the bar in place with her hands. The door withstood the shock, and shortly the danger passed for the moment, as the wildly agitated bodies rolled away.

The sounds of conflict gradually diminished

in fury as the minutes passed, until the listening girl could hear only the low grumble of worrying jaws. Finally Sally's straining ears heard a gurgling, choking sigh—and then quiet. Now her fear rose again as she wondered what might next transpire. Apprehensively she set her gaze on the window through which she half expected to see a fierce head appear as the victor inexorably returned to its first quest.

But a faint call came through the window instead. Sally's heart beat faster with joy as she recognized Jeff's voice. Then a new dread assailed her: perhaps Jeff would, all unwarned, run into whichever animal it was that had survived, and would be attacked by it! Ignoring the danger to herself in drawing the beast's attention, she approached the window and screamed a caution to Jeff, whom she could now discern running across the pasture toward the cabin. Her voice drowned out his own shouts as he raced toward her, either failing to hear her warning or choosing to ignore it.

He was without any weapon of defense and the danger into which he came plunging with great unheeding strides filled her with misgivings. A feeling that was more than anxiety, more than admiration, surged into Sally's heart. Under its prompting she turned swiftly, lifted the bar of the door, and throwing it open ran out to meet her man, to share with him the peril he was braving for her sake. She almost stumbled over the dead bear, which meant that it was the panther they had to fear.

A joyous shout greeted her. Jeff bounded forward and gathered her to him. For a moment she struggled and tried to tell him of the danger that lurked about, but he quickly reassured her. As the truth dawned upon Sally she quieted in his arms, and he held her close, this time as though by right. Into the eyes of both slowly there crept an understanding that made unnecessary the halting words Jeff had been about to utter when the buckboard collapsed, a pledge as irrevocable in the minds of these two as any ceremony.

Happy and unabashed they stood holding

each other's hands as Sally detailed her experience and Jeff explained his coming.

"I feared fer you, Sally, when I saw where you dropped the mess o' strawberries in the pasture. I'd come over to find you when I got back to the buckboard an' you wasn't there. Then I shouted an' looked all about, and saw your runnin' tracks an' the tracks of a panther. I follered them, the heart o' me sick with fear.

"When I glimpsed the buildings I see a *bear,* stretched out an' done fer alongside the door, an' I didn't know what to make of it, bein' expectant of a panther. Then I see somethin' else movin' off, an' *that* was the panther, crawlin' slow like it was jest barely alive; an' afore I looked away it rolled over an' didn't get up again. I wondered what had happened to you, with those two varmints—"

"What's that, Jeff?" interrupted Sally nervously, pressing closer to him. They listened, and heard the whining of an animal in distress, the sound strangely stifled.

"Reckon it's only another critter tryin' to

make trouble, Sally," said Jeff, lightly. In his rôle of protector to the girl who was now his he felt no doubt of his ability to conquer anything that threatened. "Does n't sound very dangerous, though. Don't be afeared." He studied the plaintive cry intently. His forest-trained ears quickly identified it. "It's a young 'un, most likely a bear cub. Let's look."

"Of course," remembered Sally. "I'd forgot about the cub I see with the mother bear when I first got to the pasture. I wonder where it can be."

Together they searched to locate its hiding-place. The whimpering calls finally drew them to the well, and looking down they saw the imprisoned baby bear.

"The poor little thing," said Sally, compassionately. "It's frightened to death—"

"Yes, an' that explains why the old she bear went for you so savage," Jeff enlightened her. "When she heard you a-runnin' toward the place she jest naturally thought 't was you dug the hole to ketch her cub an' was comin' to

kill it. Lucky you got in when you did, Sally,"
he added huskily. He knew something of the
fury of a mother bear when her cub is en-
dangered.

"Can't you get it out, Jeff?" asked Sally.
"We must n't leave it here to die."

"O' course; but I 'll have to get a rope an'
some one to help. I 'm curious about that
panther, though; let 's have a look at it first."

They followed the bloody trail of the animal
until they came to where it had fallen in its
tracks. The stark tawny form showed grim
proof of the punishment its adversary had in-
flicted, and the wonder was that the big cat
had dragged its sorely wounded, weakened
body so far. In the gaunt flanks and the
evidence of its motherhood the woodsman's
eyes read another chapter of the tragedy.

"An' now I understand somethin' else," he
said. " 'T ain't often a panther 'll attack a
human, but this one has cubs som'eres back
in the bush an' was nearly starved tryin' to
get enough food fer herself an' them. It
must 've been her mate Sam Hitchcock killed

a week back. So now there's a couple o' young ones that won't never grow up to kill sheep."

"But, oh, Jeff, we can't let those poor little kittens starve!" Sally's blue eyes grew tender with pity for the helpless cubs that doubtless were even now feeling the pangs of hunger. Before her supplicating gaze Jeff's practical point of view underwent a change.

"I reckon I'll have to hunt 'em out, Sally, if you say so," he said indulgently. "But first thing to do is to get you home to your ma; she'll be worryin' about you. Then me an' your pa can come back with a rope, an' I'll fish out the bear cub an' then back-track the panther to her den an'— What'll I do with 'em all, Sally; kill 'em to save their lives?" he grinned.

Sally was nonplussed for a moment. She hated the thought of having three innocent, cunning little wild babies killed, even if they were of the "varmint" kind. But of course it wouldn't do to turn the barn-yard into a menagerie; her father would have objections.

Then her face brightened and she beamed a shy smile at her stalwart lover.

"We could sell 'em to that collector o' wild animals for circuses who comes around, Jeff, an' buy a lot o' nice homy things"

Sally paused, blushing pinkly.

"You bet we can!" agreed Jeff, delightedly, admiration for the clever thought shining in his eyes. "You got a wonderful little head, Sally."

Jeff's delight was more for this spoken proof of the wonderful new relationship between them than for the material aspect of Sally's plan; but he added a suggestion of his own:

"Don't fergit that we got a bear-skin rug fer the house already, Sally. Pity a panther hide ain't any good in summer-time; we'd have our floor nigh covered!" He kissed her glowing cheeks.

"Let's hurry back to the road so's I can start early on my collectin'-trip," he proposed; and hand in hand they raced happily across the wild-strawberry-matted pasture.

THE FEUD ON SWIFTWATER

THE FEUD ON SWIFTWATER

A LOW-HUNG coppery sun glimmered dully through the uprearing, naked boles of pine and spruce and hemlock, laying long purplish shadows across the white-carpeted floor of the winter wood. Here and there, where a copse of juniper or young spruce spread low over the pallid surface, the shadow massed in denser tone, edged with interlaced pencilings that slowly merged into the parent gloom as the twilight deepened. As the orb approached the end of its westering the feathered life of the forest fluttered into nest or cranny or thicket, seeking safe haven from the night-prowlers that would soon be abroad. Their sleepy twitterings, blending with the languorous whisper of the trees, made a drowsy monotone that hung pleasantly on the cold, crisp air, until of a sudden it was hushed in a wave of silence as two terrifying forms came hurrying down twin aisles of the forest.

Nearly abreast and loping along at a swift pace, their approach sent the tardiest dwellers of the wood palpitatingly to cover. The larger figure, in rough homespun, rabbit-skin cap, and high moccasins thrust into the thonged hold of snowshoes, swept on as silently as the smaller, save for the crunch of his webbed foot-gear on the dry snow. The other, slightly to the rear of the man and hidden from his eyes by an artfully selected twisting path that took advantage of every tree-trunk and bush and shadow, was a squat, surly-visaged animal, reminiscent of both bear and marten. About thirty inches long, with short, powerful legs terminating in flat, hairy-soled feet, its coarse, shaggy fur of brownish black slightly relieved with a grayish cast, and a splash of clay-yellow streaking each flank and meeting at the tail, it seemed an ugly composite of several of the fur-bearers of its native wilds. Its small, dim-sighted eyes, glowering evilly from low brows fringed thickly with hair, seldom left the man as the wolverene kept pace with him by a series of seemingly awkward movements, its back arching with the curious undulations of a measuring-worm as it jumped and shambled silently through the wooded maze.

The man was returning to his cabin after an inspection of one of his trap lines, anger and humiliation writ flamingly upon his face as a result of what he had discovered, and a seething thirst for vengeance in his heart. Constantly he swept his glance to right and left as he strode along. At times he stopped suddenly and turned, freezing into immobility while he peered back along his trail. But he could discern nothing of the black, ominous shape that on each occasion shrouded itself instantly within the impenetrable gloom of tree or bush and froze into an equal movelessness. The man felt, with the sixth sense of the woodsman, that he was being followed. A faint but lively shiver traveled up and down his spine and prickled at the roots of his hair, not a sensation of fear but an uncanny and uncomfortable physical premonition that malignant eyes were following his every move. He

113

was more concerned than he liked to admit, however, for the question that persisted in his mind was whether his follower was the evil genius of his trap line or some other animal intent merely on satiating a resentful curiosity at a safe distance.

The trapper cursed his weakness in giving the matter heed, and moved over the well-packed snow at increased speed, anxious to reach his cabin and its comforts of warmth and food and rest. Without having heard the slightest sound of his companion of the trail or so much as glimpsed its sinister shadow, he emerged from the timber at the tiny clearing in the fork of two ice-bound streams, and viewed the homely portal of his hut with a grunt of relief. However unafraid of any wilding of the forest he might be, he was genuinely glad to be relieved of the oppression caused by the unseen disturbing presence. Ordinarily he would have given but little thought to the affair, but to-day he was in a mood to be annoyed, for his mind was in a perturbed state over recent happenings on his trap lines. And his growing belief that the follower, of whom his senses had warned him on several previous occasions, was no other than the author of his troubles only added to his irritation. He pictured the mean-spirited carcajou as gloating over its nefarious work at his traps and leering at him along the trail with a spiteful satisfaction at being able to worry him further by its mere proximity.

The wolverene halted at the edge of the clearing, flattening itself into perfect conceal-ment at the roots of a low-spread balsam fir. As the trapper approached the cabin he turned and shook his fist toward the black wall of trees in a mixture of anger and grim homage as he anathematized the clever miscreant who had played such havoc with his traps, and who was, he shrewdly surmised, eying him ar-rogantly from the dense growth. He was right in his conjecture, for the animal that had dogged his steps for miles and whose wicked little black eyes were appraising him mali-ciously from its hidden vantage was the same evil-dispositioned "Injun Devil" that had made a mockery of his fur-taking endeavors for several days past.

At his door the trapper scanned again the black edge of the trees and the lines of his face curved into an expression of guile. "Jest you git busy to-morrer with the traps, old feller, me boy. Mebbe ye 'll find a surprise awaitin' ye!" With which cryptic remark he entered the cabin.

Hated above all creatures of the upper fur country is the wolverene, a little brother of the bear in aspect, big cousin to the weasel and marten, and a near relative of the skunk. It is known also as "carcajou" and "Injun Devil" by the woodsmen, and called by the Indian himself "Bad dog," the ultimate term of loathing in the red man's vocabulary. Of a cunning surpassing that of the craftiest fox, on which is grafted a savage truculence that inspires it to seek trouble—or make it—it shows in all encounters with living things, human or wild, a combination of devilish ingenuity,

116

courage and strength which gives it the reputation of being the arch malefactor of the far
Northern woods. It will yield way to no
animal, save perhaps the cougar and wolf, and
of these it has but a contemptuous aversion,
for its native shrewdness is sufficient to out-
wit both in any but a claw-to-claw encounter.
And at close grips even with these powerful
enemies it is enabled by its cleverness, backed
by an indomitable courage and a strength
greater in relation to weight and size than that
of any other mammal, frequently to hold its
own. Unlovely of qualities and disposition
in a degree unequaled by all the sharers of its
environment combined, this little spawn of the
Evil One has manifold talents which make it
the most deadly efficient of the marauding
brotherhood.

When Gabe Shaddick had come to the forks
of the Swiftwater two weeks before for a season of trapping, the wolverene instantly became aware of his arrival and set itself to the
task, highly agreeable to its demon nature, of

studying the man and his methods to the end
that life should be made miserable for this
trespasser upon its domain.

Gabe's several trapping-lines, radiating fan-
like from his base, had been painstakingly
laid, the trails brushed and blazed, and the
traps, deadfalls and snares set and baited before the wolverene made its presence known.
A light fall of snow, continuing intermittently
for several days, quickly obliterated its tracks,
and without the trapper's knowledge the small,
lumbering black form had followed him on
every one of his excursions, its eyes of crafty
understanding fixed in a hateful glare upon all
his movements. When Gabe returned each
evening to his cabin the wolverene accom-
panied him at a discreet distance, halting at
the clearing's edge and observing his activities
at woodpile and stream until the trapper
closed his door for the night. Then the
watcher ended its vigil and foraged the dim
coverts for supper, soon thereafter seeking
shelter and sleep, its nocturnal habit disordered
by its bent for mischief.

Studying the man and his methods

THE FEUD ON SWIFTWATER

On several occasions Gabe had felt the weird sensation of being followed and stared at by unfriendly eyes, but he dismissed the thought contemptuously as of too little importance to bother about. Then one day he awoke swiftly to the menace that threatened his undertaking. Hardly a trap on the line that paralleled the east branch of the stream had been overlooked by a devastating agency whose tracks for the first time insolently mingled with his own and spelled plainly to the trapper the name of his opponent. With a string of sulphurous comments Gabe pursued his investigation of the ravages committed by the insatiable robber-destroyer.

A marten "set" had been neatly uncovered, the trap sprung, and the bait stolen; and apparently the wolverene had vented its displeasure on the steel contrivance, for it was so inextricably wound up with the chain that Gabe could not readily disentangle it. He kicked it aside and hurried on.

Of his next set there was nothing to be seen. A disturbance of the snow and a plentiful spattering of blood-spots, with which were mingled a few tufts of dark fur, were sufficient evidence of what had occurred. The trap was nowhere in sight. Gabe cursed his heartiest.

"Could n't even leave me the trap, drat him! That there was a prime marten fur he et up an' done me out of," he muttered. Wise in the ways of the black thief, he followed a broad trail which penetrated the brush at right angles to the line. At the distance of several rods it entered the growth of a low thick-foliaged spruce, and casting his gaze searchingly into the mass of green, Gabe was rewarded by a sight of the clog—a heavy billet of wood to which the end of the chain was fastened. Kicking off his snow-shoes, he wallowed on hands and knees to the base of the bushy tree, pulled his trap from the mound of snow under which it was buried, and backed out, with remarks appropriate to the occasion. Resetting and baiting the trap at another spot, he continued his course along the line.

His mind was now prepared for any shock of discovery. He knew how thorough an "Injun Devil" could be in its career of mischief, and he was in no wise disappointed in his expectations. For each snare and deadfall, as well as trap, had been visited by the marauder, examined with crafty eye and paw, and robbed or demolished or stolen with a most uncanny proficiency. Gabe reset such of them as were not past further usefulness, recovering one more trap from its cache, this time a hollow log; and finally arrived at the end of the line, where he halted to give full expression to his thoughts. After his first outburst he had not had time—or breath—to do justice to his outraged feelings, for his hurry to learn the worst and the repeated evidence of the wolverene's devilment had held him in a grim and silent fascination.

"Consarn yer tough hide! Ye 'd oughter have it stripped off 'n yer mean carcass alive, ye dirty, thievin', ornery black devil!" he apostrophized the absent pillager, with an added torrent of backwoods vituperation

121

which it would be unwise to spread on the records.

"I 'll git ye yet!" he growled, shaking a threatening fist aloft; and then his anger subsided as a grin persisted in breaking through the frown that seamed his face. "Ye 're a right smart varmint, sure 'nough," he conceded with reluctant admiration; "hain't no other critter can hold a candle to ye fer downright cussedness, but ye 've got a brain that some folks as I know might better swop their own fer.

"Ye hain't a-goin' to drive me off 'n my trappin'-grounds, though," he asserted. "Me an' you 'll fight this here thing out, an' see who 's boss o' the woods."

Gabe started on the trail back to camp, muttering his vexation as he went. He planned many schemes for reprisal, and during the succeeding days put them to the test, but to no avail. With a wisdom that seemed almost supernatural to the dismayed trapper his wily antagonist evidenced an ability to penetrate the secret of each well-planned trick to catch him unawares. It looked as though he must acknowledge himself beaten and take up his traps and seek some other field, as he knew others of his occupation had been forced to do in like circumstances. But the dogged nature of the backwoodsman held him to his determination to fight the affair to an issue, and the feud between man and beast continued unabated in energy and wit for the space of many weeks. And for long Gabe failed to catch even a glimpse of his rival for supremacy on the trap lines, however well planned his endeavors to surprise it at its knavery.

When on the night of his veiled threat the trapper had closed his cabin door against the deepening gloom of the woods, lighted his coal-oil lamp, and started a cheery fire, the wolverene drew back into the enveloping darkness of the forest. Hunger now assailed him, and guided to the bedding-place of a family of grouse, by a nose second to none for keenness among the forest kindred, he penetrated the tangle of thick-grown juniper, his stealthy, sinister advance carrying no warning to the sleepy birds. With the quickness of a darting snake he slashed at the huddled forms with a steel-sinewed and barbed paw. Two of the grouse were crushed to the snow, mangled past flight, the luckier ones blundering crazily to freedom through the impeding network of branches.

The merciless robber swiftly devoured his spoil. The supper finished, he licked his lips with gustatory appreciation of the delicate flesh, passed a furry black paw carefully over his broad, blunt face with a nicety of cleanliness, and looked about for a protected nook in which to sleep away the repletion of his meal. Digging away the snow from the forked roots of an adjacent tree, he settled himself comfortably in the opening and instantly dropped into slumber untroubled by any memory of his diabolical activities of the day.

At the first glimmer of dawn the wolverene emerged from his improvised den and sought his breakfast where he knew it could most easily be obtained. To wit, on one of the trap lines that had engrossed his wicked attention for so many opulent days. A close scrutiny of the trail with eye and nose, and a careful reconnoitering of the cabin, told him that the venture was safe. A weasel in its winter ermine held in the first trap occupied him for a few brief minutes, but he was too fastidious to break his fast on such stringy and musty meat when better could doubtless be found. After he had torn the distant cousin of his tribe from the steel jaws and mangled it, he proceeded up the line, and had not gone far when he sniffed the delicious odor of frozen fish.

It lay in broken bits upon the smooth surface of the snow, and the wolverene knew from past experience what this portended. He studied the layout with comprehending, savage eyes. Circling the baited area, he snatched at the outermost pieces and gulped them down. This was a breakfast much to his liking, and he craved the larger chunks that lay at the center. But his unerring instinct warned him that danger lurked beneath so tempting a feast, and that the utmost circumspection was needed to obtain it without imperiling his freedom.

With the nicest caution he advanced upon the flavory morsels, placing his feet with slow deliberation and sniffing the snow inquiringly. Suddenly he paused, for the telltale odor of iron came up to his nostrils through the powdery whiteness. He stretched out a paw and delicately scraped away the snow until the trap lay exposed, then bared his teeth in a voiceless snarl of derision and sat back upon his haunches to gloat over the unmasked fraud.

As he did so he shot into the air with an appalling screech blended of fury and fear. Half doubling upon himself in mid-jump, and alighting with savage claws outspread, he tore frantically with his fore-paws at a clinging, biting thing of steel that had seized upon his short, hairy tail with a grip as cruel as that of his own jaws. For the trapper cunningly had supplemented his main set with a second trap, which he had washed in lye and held in a smudge to destroy the scent of iron and human hands, and handled with gloves treated likewise. With infinite care to preserve the unsullied appearance of the snow surface, he had placed it where he thought the robber would stumble into it while engrossed in his designs upon the center trap. But it had hardly occurred to him that the animal would sit down upon it!

Writhing and springing about in his mad endeavors to free himself of the horrible appendage, the creature continued to claw wildly at the trap, and again and again seized it with his teeth and tried to crush it between his powerful jaws. But the awful thing clung in spite of all his efforts, and bit into the bone of his tail the harder.

Real fear entered the heart of the wolverene for perhaps the first time in his dauntless career. Arrogantly conscious of his power and devoid of any element of cowardice, he probably never before had known the sensation; but this was a horror new to his experience, and an inexplicable one, for while his sagacious brain sensed the danger of the traps of man, he had only a vague understanding of their operation. He was enlightened now, and in a manner that drove him into a blazing rage further inflamed by terror.

An impulse to flee to the familiar refuge, to which so cumbersome a thing as a trap could not be expected to follow, was acted upon with suddenness, and the animal gave a mighty bound toward the trunk of an adjacent tree. As the chain tautened against the heavy clog the trap was arrested in mid-air with a jerk that mere hair and skin could not survive, and the covering of the tail gave and slipped smoothly from the bone. The wolverene sprawled in the snow, released from the agonizing clutch, but at the expense of a smarting red tail stump.

He turned and snarled ragefully at the fearsome thing that had torn him with its teeth and was so indifferent to his own, and backed slowly off, terror still possessing him. His appetite for frozen fish was gone, and his arrogant assurance flown. He wanted nothing so much as to get away from the scene of his humiliation and pain, and to seek a shelter where he could curl up and lick the raw tail tip with healing tongue.

And his desire was heightened by the sound of gliding snow-shoes, which suddenly traveled to his ears on the thin frosty air. His glowering eyes shifted down the trail, and into them flamed an unquenchable hatred for the approaching master of the trap. For a moment his hot resentment prompted him to remain and seek to overcome his human enemy with vengeful teeth and claws; but caution dictated otherwise, and he turned reluctantly and stole silently away into the forest.

Gabe viewed the evidence of the wolverene's experience with both satisfaction and regret. The bunch of fur in the jaws of the trap made plain to him what had transpired.

"Put yer tail into it that time, did n't ye!" he chuckled, vastly pleased at the partial success of his stratagem. "Wish to blazes ye 'd put yer foot into it instead, ye thievin' varmint; there 'd be one less glutton in the woods to steal furs. Reckon that skinned tail o' yourn's givin' ye somethin' to think about, though, an' mebbe ye 'll keep away from my traps fer a spell."

Gabe's elation over having outwitted the wiliest of the forest-dwellers was added to as several days passed without further signs of the animal. Apparently the fright and pain of its experience had caused it to withdraw from the field, and he congratulated himself upon the outcome. His catch of fur increased gratifyingly, and if the take continued the accumulation of skins in his shed by Christmas time would make a sizable bale for packing into the settlement.

But the carcajou had not left the vicinity of the forks of the Swiftwater. Chastened but sullen, he kept to his old haunts, giving the trap lines, however, a wide berth, for he had no desire to try conclusions again with the trapper's devices—at least while the smart of his denuded tail reminded him of the misadventure.

THE FEUD ON SWIFTWATER

His temper, always of a surly, ungovernable quality, was if possible made more undependable by the annoyance of a tail sensitive to the slightest friction. Therefore when about a week after the frozen fish had lured him to his undoing he drifted across the zigzag trail of an animal dragging a trap and its hindering clog through the snow, he failed to be warned by the odor of wolf in the tracks and followed them in a truculent mood.

A lone timber-wolf, a pariah from some pack, ranging the coverts for grouse or rabbits, had stepped into an unbaited trap set for lynx near a rabbit runway, and its strength had enabled it to drag the heavy clog a long distance from the spot. When the wolverene drew near to the grizzled captive, whose plunging efforts to advance seemed in some way retarded, his shrewd eyes saw that the clog had become wedged between two close-growing saplings. Thereupon he climbed a tree and out upon a tangle of limbs to a point almost over the wolf, which now became aware that it was being stalked. The animal in the tree appraised the situation carefully, calmly scornful of the threatening snarls and savagely bared fangs of the one below. The green glare of the wolf's eyes and its gnashing teeth would have warned a less crafty antagonist to forbear an encounter; but the knowing little demon in the branches seemed to sense the impediment to the wolf's progress and decided that a frontal approach was safe.

He descended well beyond range of the reaching jaws and crept slowly and cautiously toward the harassed brute. The pain of the biting steel, intensified by the mad straining to advance, and the arrogant attitude of the wolverene, drove the wolf into a paroxysm of fury. But strain as it would it could not reach the annoying little beast that confronted it with such impudent calm.

Suddenly the wolverene darted in and raked a claw-studded paw across the face of his victim. The immense power of his forearm was in the slashing stroke, which laid bare the right cheek of the wolf and blinded one eye.

And then it seemed as if retribution were

to visit the insolent little scourge of the woods, for the wolf inexplicably was upon him, crushing him into the snow with the violence of its attack. The skin and tendons of its fore-foot, of which the bone was broken, lacerated and worn by the terrible struggle for liberty, had at last parted, and at the instant following the wolverene's attack the wolf had won free and launched itself upon its adversary.

The surprised trouble-seeker quickly awoke to his peril and brought all his wit and cunning into play. He would have retreated if he could, for he knew himself to be outclassed in a fair fight with a full-grown wolf; but he was given no opportunity to flee, for his foe had him down and was worrying him cruelly, its punishing jaws searching for a death hold on the black throat. The wolverene luckily succeeded in wriggling over on his back, the better to bring his saberlike claws into play, and with them he raked the belly of the wolf with a terrible energy that no living thing could long endure.

The fresh strength of the chunky little ani-

mal gave him an advantage over the larger
and heavier beast, for the wolf's staying
powers had been sapped by its long struggle
with the trap. Also it was losing blood from
the dismembered leg and torn cheek, and was
further handicapped by its blindness on one
side. Had it not been for these factors the
result of the wolverene's temerity would doubtless have been fatal to him; but luck favored
him, for the wolf's vitality was ebbing fast,
while his own was scarcely impaired. He was
wounded in many places by the sharp rending
teeth on which the wolf mainly depended for
offense, but had managed by shrinking his upper body into a compact mass to evade the
seizure of his throat, the coarse, thick fur making a grip difficult; while all during the struggle his own terrible weapons were desperately
employed. From the purchase of hooked fore-
paws set deep into the crowding shoulders,
his fast-working hinder feet tore with cruel
eviscerating strokes at the wolf's vitals; and
the punishment was telling on the larger animal.

THE FEUD ON SWIFTWATER

Its stamina inferior to the wolverene's through the force of circumstances, the wolf's chances were appreciably waning. As the vigor of its efforts subsided the other redoubled his exertions, and taking advantage of a second's cessation in the enemy's onslaught, twisted violently from his position and regained his feet. The wolf sprang to recover its advantage, but the wolverene was quicker. Evading the move, and flanking the other's rush, he secured a hold on its throat that no striving could loosen. With a tenacity as inexorable as that of locked steel, he held on in spite of the threshing endeavors of the wolf to throw him off, his jaws working steadily inward. At last they met, severing the air passage and veins, and the gray-furred form sank into the snow, the savage gleam in its eyes slowly glazing in death.

The wolverene had had his fill of bloody work, and after a few questioning snaps at the limp form withdrew from the scene without obeying the promptings of his nature to mangle the conquered foe. The dreadful gashes that

135

covered him were distressingly evident now
that the lust for battle was sated, and his
racked body craved shelter where he could lie
and lick his wounds. He dragged himself
painfully to a fissure high up in a ledge of
rock a short distance off, and there remained
for nearly a week, nursing his hurts. He went
foodless for a few days, leaving the den only
to seize a mouthful of snow when his throat
craved moisture; and his cooled blood and
the clear untainted air of the forest performed
their miracle of quick healing. With returning strength he ventured forth at dark and
stalked the thickets for whatever small game
they harbored.

Meanwhile Gabe had discovered that his
blind set had been sprung and trap and clog
carried away by an animal that had not figured
in his plans. He followed the plain trail of
the wolf, and coming upon its torn body read
in the evidence before his eyes the story of the
wolverene's exploit.

"Blamed if the little cuss ain't still hangin'
round and sp'ilin' my furs!" he grumbled in

a mixture of disgust and admiration. "He's sure a gritty little devil to tackle a wolf, even if it was ketched in a trap. Looks like somethin' happened that he had n't figgered on, though, an' I reckon it was only his smartness that got him off."

Gabe surmised that the victor had holed up to recover from its wounds, and hoped that at last a chance offered for taking it at a disadvantage and ridding the woods of the elusive black pest. He followed the wolverene's blood-marked trail to the base of the ledge, but on reaching it realized that no human could scale its face. Grinning ruefully at this checkmate, he returned to the trap line, his feelings of assurance over the future gone. The wolf pelt that he had expected to return with had not been worth stripping, which added to his chagrin; but he took the head for the sake of the bounty.

When the wolverene's hurts were fully mended and his old-time arrogance had returned to him, his restored body craved stronger food than had sustained him during his healing.

Rabbits and grouse and wood mice were delicate titbits, but weak food as a steady diet. He wanted rich red meat, and on happening across a deer trail in the early dawn his hunger for venison became overpowering.

The tracks smelled comparatively fresh, but the wolverene knew better than to attempt to run down the fleet-footed deer. Selecting a leaning tree a branch from which overhung the trail, he ascended it and crawled out along the limb, flattening himself upon it above the runway. Here he remained for hours in absolute immobility except for his roving eyes, which peered expectantly up and down the approaches. Once a wolverene assumes this attitude of waiting for game, no lapse of time can discourage him and nothing of lesser consequence than his expected quarry can lure him from his perch. His confidence that sooner or later a deer is certain to appear along a deer runway seems to sustain him, and doubtless his philosophy is well founded.

Not until the sun had mounted in the cloudy winter sky and the wolverene's hunger nearly past endurance was his patience rewarded. A fine antlered buck came stepping down the trail, quivering nostrils alert for the smell of danger, but all unwarned of the crouching terror that awaited him, for the wolverene's scent did not fall to the lower level of air. As the buck passed below the limb the black form fell like a stone upon its back. The deer snorted with terror and pain as the needlelike claws sank into his flesh, and bounded into the air in a series of plunges that would have shaken off a less determined rider. Then he darted in among the trees, striving to scrape off the clinging horror; but unsuccessful in this and crazed with fear, returned to the familiar trail, down which he raced with panic-stricken leaps. All the while, despite the violent rocking of his seat, the wolverene's ravening teeth were sawing into the deer's neck, seeking the jugular vein.

Now it chanced that the trapper's supply of fresh meat had run low and he had selected this same day in which to re-stock his larder with venison. With his rifle he was still-hunting a cleft in the hardwood ridge when the sound of a flying deer came to his hearing. He awaited its approach with weapon ready for a snap shot, and wondered what pursuing enemy it was that drove it at such speed. As the rocketing animal flashed across his vision he fired, aware at the instant that the enemy was not pursuing but was aboard! The deer faltered at the shot, plunged on for a few broken strides, and fell sprawling in the snow, shot through the heart. Gabe ran forward, curious to know the nature of its burden, and was amazed and elated as he saw the wolverene slip from the crimsoned back of the deer and glide off into the brush. He fired at the vanishing black shape, but too late, and cursing his tardiness sent an exultant shout after the vanquished fellow hunter.

"Drive a deer up to me, will ye, when ye knew I was sp'ilin' fer a haunch o' venison!" he taunted. "Well, ye're a fergivin' little cuss, an' this squares ye fer clawin' up a prime wolf pelt fer me. Leastways I've got the meat, whether ye meant it fer me or no, an' I'm thankful to ye."

He drew his knife to sever the veins of the neck, but this was hardly necessary, for the wolverene had at last reached the jugular and the hot blood already was melting a deep red pocket in the snow. It was clear to Gabe that the deer soon would have weakened from loss of blood and fallen beneath its savage incubus, had he not fortuitously stepped into the affair.

The buck was full grown and too heavy to be carried whole to the cabin, and Gabe concluded to make two loads of it. He skinned and dressed it and divided the carcass. The fore part he carried some distance off the trail and hung by the antlers in the fork of a tree-limb. Making a sling of the skin in which he wrapped the other half, he threw this over his shoulder and started for camp, feeling reasonably certain that the wolverene's fear of the rifle shots would drive it afar and prevent its return to the spot for at least a few hours; and he intended to hurry back and secure the remaining meat before its appetite and returning courage drew the glutton back, or any other enterprising prowler could steal it.

But Gabe reckoned without the animal's growing disdain for a human who seemed impotent actually to harm it. Its dulled memory had long since disassociated the man from its mishap with the trap, and growing familiarity with his activities had bred in it a contemptuous tolerance that was dispelled only by the trapper's direct approach. It had been frightened by the abrupt ending of its quarry's career at the man's hand, and the shot at itself that followed sent it in angry fear well into the depths of the forest. But the fright was short-lived, and the creature's courage and defiance returned with dawning comprehension that it was in no wise harmed in body by the man's act. Quietly it slunk back to the scene of the killing and drew near while Gabe was still engaged with the carcass.

With bared teeth it snarled soundlessly at the tantalizing spectacle. No other indignity is quite so deeply resented by the wild forest

folk as that of being robbed of their prey, and
the wolverene lay in its concealment working
itself into a frenzy of hate and rage. Several
times it darted forward a few paces, as though
to rush upon the despoiler, and as often drew
back, the fear that arose within it in the near
presence of the man overcoming its inclination.

When Gabe shouldered his burden and de-
parted, the wolverene advanced cautiously and
followed him for a short distance; then, satisfied that he was leaving, returned and ranged
warily about the spot, suspicious of a trap.
It disdained the entrails, for nothing less than
solid, hearty meat would satisfy it. Coming
up beneath the hanging fore-quarters of the
deer, it studied the ground and tree with minute scrutiny for many minutes. This looked
decidedly like a baited trap, and caution and
fierce hunger strove for mastery. Finally its
voracity conquered, the appetizing smell of
fresh venison overpowering its prudence. It
could not reach the meat from below, and
climbed the tree to try to dislodge the wedged

antlers, unheedful of the possibility of the man's reappearance.

Biting and clawing savagely at the antlers in its impatience, the wolverine failed to note the trapper's return until it was startled by the close sound of his approach. He was not yet in sight, but was making his way slantingly up the side of the gully, his snow-shoes difficult to manage on a climb.

The hair rose along its back in impotent anger at this final balking of its appetite. But it dared not linger, and glaring furiously toward the oncoming man it shrank back along the limb, that it might descend and flee into the shadows.

Then a vengeful impulse to bring into play an evil power of pollution which the wolverene possesses in common with the skunk, caused it to run forward along the branch and discharge the nauseous secretion of its oil-sacs over the meat. Having defiled the flesh beyond consumption by any but its own tribe, it slid hastily down the tree and faded into the surrounding gloom.

144

THE FEUD ON SWIFTWATER

As Gabe drew close to the cache his nostrils apprised him of the near presence of his rival, and he wondered idly what had caused it to corrupt the air with its malodor, and with deeper interest if it had stolen the suspended deer meat. The evident quick return of the wolverene did not greatly astonish him, for he was prepared for any upset of his theories concerning this bewildering animal personality. He hurried to the tree, where the quarters still hung apparently untouched; but when he drew below the branch he was enlightened as to what had occurred.

"Consarn the critter, if he ain't gone and sp'iled the meat I scairt him away from!" Gabe exploded, sniffing his disgust at the fetid smell. " 'Tain't no good to nobody now, savin' the critter hisself, an' I 'll be blamed if I 'll leave it fer him, the ornery skunk!"

Holding his breath, he lifted the meat from its place, and attaching to the antlers a length of copper wire which he carried for snares, he dragged the corrupted flesh to the nearest branch of the Swiftwater. With his hand-ax he chopped a hole in the ice and shoved it through into the stream.

"That 'll leave ye hungry, I reckon," he muttered vindictively, "an' give ye a chance to work yer deviltry some other way. Ye've done me out of a fine chunk o' venison, but I 've got the whip-hand of ye, fer never a bite o' the deer will ye get, savin' the innards, which ye 're welcome to."

Gabe retired to his shack and cooked himself a prodigious supper of deer liver, which tasted surprisingly better than usual. He talked much to an imaginary presence, gloating over the adventure of the afternoon, for to the solitary woodsman there was a growing need of companionship and conversation. And the long-drawn contest with the "Injun Devil" satisfied this craving in a large measure; he would now have felt unutterably lonely without the constant clashing of wit with the animal, which continued unabated through the ensuing weeks.

The wolverene soon was back at its old pastime of interference with the traps, and only by the exercise of sharpened ingenuity could Gabe achieve a reasonable catch. He shortened the old lines and laid new ones, and as the robber could not be in all places at once, the trapper gathered a modest harvest of furs, though far too small to pay him for his efforts.

A week before Christmas he decided that he would not brave the gibes of the settlement folk by exhibiting his small catch and explaining the cause. The explosive backwoods mirth that would greet his story of having been outwitted by an "Injun Devil" would be galling; and he knew he would be unable to conceal the facts. A small catch on the Swiftwater forks, which were known to be a rich trapping-ground, would entail explanations, and bitter as the true one would be, the alternative of acknowledging himself incompetent on the trap line would be far worse. No, he would await the breaking up of winter to take his furs in, and trust to a large measure of success during the coming months, perhaps with the marauder disposed of.

The craving for a respite in his ceaseless

work and vigilance was born of this renunci-
ation.   He had dwelt vaguely at times on the
advisability of shifting his base to a trapping-
ground higher up on the West Branch; and
without seriously considering the change—for
he was determined that he would not be the one
to be driven from the Forks—he thought to
make a casual view of this section an excuse
for a brief absence from his labors.   As soon
as he determined upon this he made up a small
pack, banked his fire, and shutting his cabin
tight against intruders set forth with ax and
rifle for the upper waters of the branch.

The wolverene marked his going.   The man
seemed to ignore his traps strangely, and the
animal trailed him curiously to the boundaries
of the grounds.   There it lay watching for a
time, then slouched back to the traps and pursued its usual tactics along the line.   It drew
near to the clearing at dusk, and peered from
the wall of trees at the cabin, which seemed
deserted.   The trapper did not appear by
nightfall, and the wolverene lingered at its
post far into the night in vague puzzlement.

In the early dawn of the morning it again studied the camp. Clearly the man had not returned. Its keen nose, vastly more dependable than its dull-sighted eyes, could catch no human scent. It circled the clearing and could discover no fresh tracks, and little by little drew closer to the cabin. When it reached the log structure the animal's boldness had grown with its rising assurance that the man had deserted his den. Here indeed was a long-sought opportunity to investigate the strange dwelling-place of its enemy, perhaps to despoil it.

The wolverene searched for an entrance, sniffing and scratching at the door and along its base at front and back, the sides being obstructed by the trapper's stacked supply of firewood. The fur-shed at the rear was equally impregnable, for while it was constructed with a view of admitting plenty of air, the animal could not squeeze through the openings. Had it been so disposed it could have cut through the logs beaverwise, but it seemed to understand that this was not the real lair of the human. A tiny window high up on one side of the cabin was protected by a stout slab shutter, which resisted its efforts to tear it loose. The wolverene had climbed to it on the pile of wood, and from the spruce thatch that covered the stack it was an easy jump to the peaked roof.

It scraped away the snow and dug at the "scoops" with which the hut was roofed, dislodging a quantity of mud chinking; but it could not break through. At last its attention was drawn to the chimney of stone and clay, and this provided an easy way in. It slipped quickly down the rough interior. At the bottom a sheet of tin gave instantly to its weight and it sprang clear of the heap of hot ashes in the fireplace and was in the cabin.

Here was a rich field for the gratification of its chief passions—gluttony, prying and destruction. The larder first attracted it, and it reveled in Gabe's supplies of salt pork, flour, molasses and dried apples, breaking into the sacks and pails gleefully and stuffing its capacious stomach nearly to bursting. Then with the abandon of a mischievous monkey loosed in a toy-shop it began its career of ruin throughout the cabin. Gabe's bunk was despoiled of its balsam mattress and the tips scattered over the floor; every article of bedding and clothing was torn into shreds, moccasins chewed into a pulpy mass, and spare snowshoes denuded of their webs. Nothing was overlooked by the efficient little demon in its lust for destruction and vengeance. A high shelf drew its attention, and in clutching at what it held pulled over a tin of coal-oil, drenching itself with the contents. The evil-smelling fluid was annoying and the wolverene scrubbed its fur against the log walls and wallowed in the litter that covered the floor; but the odorous stuff still clung tenaciously.

At this moment it was startled into an attitude of strained hearing by a faint, familiar sound that caused its fur to bristle in anger and fear. There was no mistaking the significance of that dry crunching of snow that grew more and more distinct as the trapper, returning from an even briefer journey than he had contemplated, strode up to the cabin.

151

At a point only a little beyond the boundaries of his lines Gabe had camped for the night, and in the early morning had repented of his neglect of his duties for a cruise of which there was no vital need. And he had hurried back to his base, regretting the weakness that had prompted him to leave.

In a panic the wolverene leaped for the chimney as Gabe neared the hut. But unaccountably the tin sheet that had given way so easily when it entered now presented a smooth, inexorable barrier.

Gabe's chimney had proved highly efficient as to "draft," so much so that to retain the warmth of his fire when it was reduced to coals he had fashioned a damper from a flattened molasses tin. This, hung on a wire transfixed in the chimney throat so that the smaller weighted part caused the larger section to rise and impinge on a nail driven in the stone, thus closing the passage, gave the cabin the full benefit of the heat. When Gabe wished the chimney to draw, a small chain attached to the lip of the damper enabled it to be lowered and fastened to a nail set in below. The damper had been left closed when Gabe shut up the cabin, the better to preserve the warmth during his absence; and it had fortuitously played the part of a trap-door.

When the wolverene sprang confidently for the opening it was repulsed by the tin obstruction and fell sprawling into a heap of ash-covered coals in the fireplace. Scattered by its fall and fanned into flickering light by the violence of its movements, the embers instantly ignited the oil soaked fur of the animal. Enveloped in flames and squealing pitiably, it rushed about the cabin, leaving a blazing trail in the debris that it had so effectively prepared for its work of arson.

The weird sounds that came from the cabin as Gabe reached the entrance moved him to lift the latch without the delay of removing his snow-shoes. As he opened the door he was driven back in horrified wonder as a blast of flame and smoke smote him in the face. And at the instant an animated streak of fire dashed between his legs, nearly upsetting him, and madly circled about in the snow, emitting screeches of agony.

The trapper's bewilderment was succeeded by partial understanding. The flaming thing that plunged crazily about the clearing quickly lost its cometlike appearance, and became a scorched and smoking animal nearly denuded of its fur—unquestionably his enemy, the wolverene.

He raised his rifle and ended the beast's suffering; then he turned his attention to the cabin which, with its contents, he saw, was doomed. He rushed around to the rear, where his fur-shed joined it, and discovered to his relief that it had not yet been reached by the flames. Kicking off his snow-shoes and entering, he salvaged his precious skins, getting all of them out before the fire reached the structure.

Gabe's relief at having saved his fur tempered his regret for the burning of his cabin and its contents. Fur represented money, the wherewithal to buy new possessions to replace those burned. The destruction of the pelts, virtually his wages for many weeks of lonely toil, would have been a backwoods tragedy. To replace the cabin meant only a few days of labor. The loss of his belongings, while serious to a man in the depths of the forest, was not in the present instance a disaster, for luckily he had the equipment carried on his short trip, which was sufficient for all immediate needs. While but little food remained in his pack, his rifle would provide meat until he could re-outfit.

He went around the still blazing logs and stood over the blistered remains of what had been his arch tormentor for so long a period. Turning the body over with his foot he examined its tail. The tip was a bald knob of skin-covered bone.

"It's sure enough me old friend," Gabe addressed the stark form. "There would n't 've been room fer another like ye on the Forks, that's sartin. Ye're past further devilment, which is where I've wanted ye this long time; but the honors ain't with me, fer ye're dead through no wit o' mine, an' ye sure had yer innings with me afore ye went. I 'm regretful ye had to go in such pain.

" 'T is you that got in the last lick, ye obstinate little blackleg, fer ye 've drove me off the grounds; an' ye willed I 'd go in to the Christmas doin's at the post, whether I would or no!" he concluded grimly; and set out to gather his traps and snare wires.

Later in the day, drawing a crudely wrought sledge of poles fastened together with wire, on which was bound his all-too-small bundle of furs, the trapper started on the long and toilsome march to the settlement.

THE SURVIVAL

THE SURVIVAL

OUTWARDLY the age-old pine presented a sturdy appearance, its bark unriven, its spreading crown a majesty of glossy blackish green towering above its lesser neighbors high into the vast cobalt dome. But its once iron heart was sore with the ravages of myriads of borers that had cut through and through the fibers of its very soul, working their greater havoc lower in the bole, where the strain of its stand against the buffetings of Northern winter winds was greatest. In its arrogant growth it had crowded out many aspiring seedlings, and the little park it had made for itself offered an ideal site for a forest-dweller's shelter, a vantage that had not escaped the eye of a cruising backwoodsman; and a small cabin occupied the spot, built by him and his trapping partner for use during the fur season.

159

Through the long boreal night the steely glitter of stars thickly sown in a low-hung, blue-black sky evoked an answering sparkle from the crusted snow that blanketed the upper branches of the king pine and added not insignificantly to the strain at its roots. This night the frigid air assailed the thriftiest of the trees, and the complaining of overwrought wood punctuated the faint whisper of the forest with a sound like the snapping of tense iron. To the old pine the inexorable cold was the final influence that determined the span of its life. Its already weakened fibers, drawn taut beyond their power to rally by the intense air, began to part in a crescendo of pistol-like reports. As the rigidity of the lofty column was steadily being threatened by the severing of its wooden thews, a vagrant blast of wind reached down from the Arctic and pushed its icy weight against the overburdened crown. The pine shuddered with the impact and strove to resume the perpendicular with its old elasticity, but miserably failed in the attempt.

The sharp musketry of rending wood rever-

berated through the forest aisles as the giant
tree swayed and broke; but as the branching
top in the arc of its fall encountered its fellows
—smashing, grinding, breaking through the
mass of living green—the mounting thunder of
its descent drowned out the lesser sound, as
well as the anguished cry that arose from
beneath the tiny cabin that lay in the path of
its destruction.

Dave MacWhirter's repose that night had
been untroubled by the familiar forest noises,
and he was sleeping the sleep of a healthily
tired trapper who had covered the line of his
traps during a two-days' absence from his
base. But the loud cracking of wood at the
roots of the old pine during its death-throes
brought him out of his slumber with a sense
of impending danger, and he had quickly
slipped from his bunk, seized his rabbit-skin
cap and hand-ax by instinct, and was emerging
from the doorway when the trunk of the tree
crashed down upon his hut. Instantly he was
pinned to the ground, and in the middle of a

yell wrung out of him by the sudden horror
was made unconscious by a blow upon the head
from a thrashing branch. His senses returned
in a few minutes under the urge of the stinging cold, and he awoke to a knowledge of his
plight. The fierce, pulsing ache in his left
leg told him that it was broken; it was wedged
fast at the ankle between the uprights of the
door-casing that had sheared together when
the hut collapsed. Dave knew that if he were
held in the jaws of that trap for only a brief
space he would perish with the cold that even
now was searching his veins with chill insist-
ence. The analogy of his position to that of
the animals he found in his own traps occurred to him, and his lips twisted momently in
a bitter smile.

"I reckon as how I got myself ketched fer
fair, this trip," he thought aloud. "All it
needs to make it seem lifelike is fer a critter to
come amblin' along and set up on its hind legs
an' grin at me, an' then fetch me a bat over the
head."

As the trapper grimly cogitated upon his

chances he noted thankfully that the iron blackness of the night was fading to the gray of first dawn; and when the steel-blue preludial light had filtered through the forest maze he was cheered by the awakening life of the tree-dwellers, alert to greet the first glittering promise of day. A squirrel ran along the trunk of the fallen pine and chattered at Dave his disapproval of what he doubtless considered a wanton act of the human interloper. A tiny animated ball of sober gray feathers piped its "*tsic-a-dee-dee-dee*" companionably in the upper limbs of a near-by spruce. Heartened by the breaking of the grim silence by these least dwellers of the solitude, and inspired by the gloriously breaking day, the mind of the woodsman turned more hopefully to its task.

His partner, Gabe Shaddick, might return the next day, or the one following, dependent upon his luck in getting through. Gabe had left the camp two days before for the trader's store at Little Gap, with a small bale of furs to be exchanged for needed provisions. Granting that Dave could free himself, could

163

he survive the harshness of the Northern winter, in his shelterless and cruelly hurt condition, until Gabe arrived? Inability to loosen the scissorlike grip of the door timbers meant certain death within a few hours, for his necessarily restricted efforts to keep his blood circulating would not long suffice to ward off the clutching fingers of the cold. But he resolutely refused to consider this possibility; by some means or other he would win free, to pit his craft and will against the hostile forces of the wild.

Luckily Dave's habit was to wear most of his clothes through the night in winter weather; in fact, this night he had even donned his mackinaw, which with his heavy garments of homespun would preserve him against instant annihilation by the pitiless frost. His cowhide larrigans, worn while he was about his household duties, he had kicked off on going to his bunk, but because of the unusual frigidity he had drawn on in their stead his highly prized sealskin *muk luks,* of soft-tanned pelts with the fur side turned in; and to this fortunate chance he owed the preservation of his feet. He remembered that he had seized his ax as he sprang for the door, and he was able to find it after a brief search. His hands already were stiffening, and pawing around with them in the snow made it almost impossible for him to grip the helve; but by beating them on his mackinaw and thrusting them inside his shirt against his body he restored them to a semblance of strength. He recalled with a pang that upon his arrival at the cabin he had as usual withdrawn his thick woollen mittens from his coat, through the sleeves of which they were reeved with a cord when in use; and the question of the moment was how to keep his hands from freezing. He could spare them least in his endeavors to extricate himself from the wooden jaws that were biting savagely into his ankle.

The trapper's plight was desperate, for no living thing that lacked its full powers of physical action could survive long under exposure to the merciless cold that held the wilderness in its grip. But it takes much to daunt the heart of a woodsman, and he would not dwell on the almost certain outcome of his mishap. Puzzlement over the cause of the big pine's fall mingled in Dave's mind with a sense of personal grievance at the scurvy trick the apparently sound tree had played him. Skilled in forest ways and able to see, or even to sense, an impending windfall, he instinctively avoided the vicinity of any threatening tree when establishing his camp. But the secret of the king pine had eaten at its heart and shown no outward scars that the eyes of the keenest woodsman could detect; and even Dave's intuition had been impotent against this perfidy of nature.

A momentary review of the happening recalled to his stoic mind the cry that pain and terror of the unknown force that bore him down had wrung from him while he was still clouded with sleep. A hot surge of shame for the weakness glowed through the stubble of his cheeks, for both human and wild denizens of the timbered wastes are schooled to suffer their pangs in silence, except in the last extremity.

"I did n't have no call to squeal like a baby," he admitted to himself, "even if a durn big stick did give me a whack that like to broke my skull. But it sure knocked the sand out of me fer a moment!" With an oath of self-reproach he brought his mind back to the question of liberating himself.

The problem of his hands was no less serious than that of his imprisoned foot, and Dave beat them violently against his body in an effort to restore them to power. But he realized the futility of this, for the cold deprived him effectually of their help: keeping them from freezing prevented him from using them to free himself; using them would result almost immediately in freezing them stiff. A qualm of despair arose within him as he contemplated the issue; but his habit of calm thought quickly reasserted itself and banished it.

His awkward posture made his efforts tiring, and to rest his arms he thrust his hands into the pockets of his coat. As he did so he gave a yell so piercing that a passing butcher-bird, alighting in a near-by fir to examine the phenomenon of this human creature caught in a trap, gave a startled squawk and blundered crazily among the snow-laden branches in its mad haste to depart.

As Dave drew forth his coveted mittens he indulged in a burst of whimsical profanity, addressed impartially to his forgetfulness of having placed them there, his failure to try his pockets earlier, and his glad relief at finding them. Always he had hung them on a nail to dry on entering the cabin—on every occasion but this, when some whim of preoccupation, or laziness, had prompted him to stuff them into his pocket. Gratefully he drew them on, passing the connecting cord around his neck, and again turned his attention to the matter of freeing his foot, which was aching horribly. A tentative chop with the ax at the topmost timber resulted as he had feared: the sharp agony it caused his fractured leg made that method of escape impossible.

THE SURVIVAL

Suddenly Dave became aware of a familiar smell mingling with the resinous fragrance of the early morning air. He sniffed distrustfully, a vaguely defined fear taking form in his mind. He glanced apprehensively into the chaos of splintered, broken wood, and the fear crystallized into a deadly certainty. For a spiral of tenuous blue arose from the tumbled heap as he looked. Other spirals joined it, and grew into thick columns, and these with incredible swiftness became a choking, eye-smarting billow of smoke. Then came a premonitory crackling, and following close upon the sound licking yellow tongues appeared and snapped and hissed about the pitchy living bark of the pine where it lay across the ruins. The dying embers of the sheet-iron stove, spilled out in the sudden destruction, had gained renewed life from the tiny drafts that eddied through the crevices of the pile, and stubbornly smoldering for a time, had at last ignited the seasoned wood.

Dave's ruddy face lost some of its color as he watched. And to the dread of this new menace was added the poignant thought that his food supply was doomed.

There would be no time now to work at the door timbers with the ax, slowly and with infinite care lest he break the helve, in the hope of prying them apart. He knew he could accomplish nothing by sudden, strong pressure, and besides, this would endanger his ax—that most jealously guarded of all a woodsman's possessions, and invaluable to one at bay with Nature.

The flames spread and mounted higher in the thin, cold air, and the heat, at first grateful to the chilled flesh of the woodsman, now began to prickle the skin of his face. As the snapping, crackling flames came creeping inexorably closer, his woollen clothing gave forth a faint elusive steam, and, drying out, began to singe, with the acrid smell of burning cloth.

In a panic of horror as the heat became intolerable, Dave wrenched savagely with his wedged leg, but desisted from this useless effort with a groan as the pain of tortured flesh and sinew and bone cleared his brain. Frantically he seized handfuls of snow and hurled it into the flames that now were nearing the timbers which anchored him to the pile; but it only sputtered weakly, powerless to stay their advance. With hope nearly gone, Dave suddenly bethought himself of the abandoned expedient; and this he determined to risk in his desperation. Groping for his ax, he seized it and inserted the head between the locked timbers. Gathering his strength, he was about to exert a prying force that would have snapped the tough hickory as though it had been matchwood; but the pressure that promised ruin to his precious ax was stayed in the nick of time. For the ridge-pole of the cabin, across one end of which lay the fallen pine, and whose other end bore down upon the upper of the two door pieces, thus transmitting to them the weight of the tree, suddenly burned through midway of its length; and the wooden jaws opened.

Scorched and smoking, and with strength nearly gone from the reaction, Dave rolled over and, the ax still gripped in one hand, slowly dragged himself away from the reaching flames; and still within the circle of their heat, propped himself against a small, low-boughed balsam fir. Reaching up with his ax, he hacked off the nearest branches and managed awkwardly to draw them beneath him. Half reclining, with his hurt leg extended straight before him on the cushion of balsam boughs, Dave resolved to rest there in the warmth until the fire burned itself out. The flames already were licking up the door timbers. They swept on greedily, devouring the debris of the hut as though intent on making complete in the shortest possible space of time the devastation begun by the traitorous pine.

Although the fire had been the means of setting Dave free, it exacted a heavy price for the service, for when it had finished its work it had consumed everything in the cabin that might have served the woodsman in his extremity. Even his whole cutting of fire-wood was gone, for he had stacked it up, for the sake of convenience, against the side of the hut.

THE SURVIVAL

As Dave had emptied his pockets of their heavier contents and removed his belt before turning in, he was unprovided with knife or matches, the latter having been contained in a waterproof metal box of some bulk. He was also without the solace of tobacco, for his pipe and big black plug of "smoking and chewing" had been laid aside at the last moment before he sank into sleep. Aside from his fortunately complete outfit of clothing he had only his ax, almost miraculously preserved to him.

As the flames died to a feeble spluttering, the returning chill warned Dave that he must exert himself. He was becoming conscious of hunger and thirst, now that the excitement had worn off. But the most pressing need was the binding up of his leg, for the slightest movement disturbed the fracture and almost unnerved him with the agony.

Any skillful woodsman is a competent first-aid practitioner, and Dave was no bungler at backwoods surgery. Luckily it was a simple fracture with which he had to deal. With slow, methodical movements, in order to avoid agitating the broken bone, he drew from beneath him the cushion of fir branches, trimmed several of them, and after cutting off a foot of the larger end of each, split the sticks lengthwise. Bending over, and working at some disadvantage because of the thick covering of wool and sealskin, he manipulated the muscles of his broken leg until the edges of the fracture locked, his teeth grinding with the torture. Then he straightened up and sat for a moment drawing into his lungs great gulps of air and wiping the sweat-beads from his forehead.

When he had overcome the nausea brought on by his Spartan effort, he laid the splints about the leg and bound them tightly with the cord from his mittens. There was not enough of this to hold them permanently in place, and making long withes by twisting the remaining lengths of the fir branches and knotting them together, he wrapped this primitive rope around and around the splint-covered leg, finally achieving a very serviceable cast. The operation had been a slow and laborious one, for he was compelled to work without his mittens, and it was necessary for him to replace them at short intervals and beat his hands furiously upon his chest to restore the nearly congealed blood to activity.

Having accomplished his surgery and regained control over his outraged nerves, he dragged himself nearer to the glowing bed of coals that was all that remained of his wilderness lodge, and seated himself upon the log that had been his chopping-block. This had lain just outside the zone of the flames, and Dave found it a vastly more comfortable seat than the snow-covered ground under the fir. The coals sparkled and snapped in the frosty air, and the flame-eaten bole of the pine at its juncture with them smoldered and smoked, its living wood having resisted total destruction. Here Dave resolved to linger for a time, to soak in the vivifying warmth and gather strength for the ordeal before him.

Thirst was his immediate problem. The stream that ran through a deep gully near by provided the cabin with water in open weather and ice for melting during the frozen period; but while Dave might have managed the descent, he knew he would be unable to return up the steep bank. His throat and tongue were dry from long abstinence, aggravated by shock and anxiety; but with snow all about him he had restrained the natural impulse to eat it and allay the craving. For it is known to those wise in the lore of the open that the eating of snow by a woodland derelict to quench thirst is somewhat akin in its effects to the drinking of sea water by an ocean castaway. Dave knew in an elemental way that unmelted snow makes one thirstier, and that continued indulgence thus fostered results in dangerous chilling of the body. A more scientific mind than his could have told that the cause of this lies in the presence of ammonia and other gases which, gathered from the air by the flakes in their fall, have a tendency to dry up the secretions, thereby intensifying the thirst. But being of volatile nature, these gases are driven off instantly by heat; and therefore, when Dave sought for some method of melting snow to quench his thirst he obeyed a rule of chemistry of which he had never heard.

He was at a loss for the means until his search uncovered a scrap of half-rotted birch-bark, the last vestige of his kindling-supply, tucked under the far side of the log. From this he fashioned a rude cup, discouragingly small and fragile. Given a piece of birch-bark and a sliver of wood, the woodsman of parts can provide a competent vessel for almost any purpose; but Dave's fragment was nearly past usefulness and threatened to fall apart with handling.

He filled the cup with snow and held it over a heap of glowing embers, nursing it carefully with both hands. As the snow melted it sagged and leaked and Dave barely had time to lift it to his lips and drain it of what water remained before it fell apart. His thirst was far from satisfied, but he had eased the craving of his throat for moisture, and with this he was philosophically content.

The hunger gnawing at his vitals became more poignant with the puny draught, and the demands of his starved tissues grew in intensity with the passing of the minutes; for the body fires of the timber folk of Northern latitudes burn briskly, and require hearty and generous fuel to keep them well stoked.

The morning was now far advanced. The hard gold of the mounting sun held promise of little warmth, though the wind had subsided somewhat with the coming of day. The activities of the smaller woodland folk—those that by custom remained to brave the rigors of the Northern winter, and did not hibernate—increased as the day wore on. Dave drew a measure of comfort from this, for though callous, in pursuit of his vocation, to the hurt of the fur-bearers, he felt the fellowship of the true woodsman for all animal life. Snow-buntings flashed and twittered through the interlacing branches above him as he crouched in the dying heat, and gladdened him with their friendly sallies from the treetops to investigate the curiously inert figure seated on the log. With a stick he poked about in the ashes, hoping against hope to discover some article of food not wholly beyond salvage; but he was rewarded only by the occasional charred evidence of his once ample stores, reduced to cinders and falling into blackened dust at his touch. The few cooking-utensils he and Gabe possessed had fused into an unrecognizable mass; and he could find no trace of his knife.

He thought longingly of the cache made by him and Gabe at the farther limits of their line of traps, which extended in a rough circle of far-reaching dimensions. Here they had been wont to camp for the night in a bark wickiup when the catch was plentiful enough to delay completing the rounds; and here was hearty food a-plenty, but at too sickening a distance for him to contemplate reaching it. He thought, too, of the supplies that Gabe was even now packing swiftly over the snowy trail; and he whimsically dwelt on his partner's bewilderment at the sight that would meet his eyes when he arrived.

"Reckon Gabe's eyes 'll pop out like a rabbit's with a weasel runnin' it, when he get a look at what's left of the cabin," he observed, and chuckled at the thought, his indomitable courage enabling him to perceive humor in the situation.

His ravening hunger finally drove him to a course that gradually had taken form in his mind, repulsive though it was. The nearest trap was a scant half-mile from the camp base, and to this he would drag himself, if his strength held, and eat of its catch—granted that it held a catch. If it did not, then his fate was in the hands of whatever forest gods there be that influence the destiny of the wildwood dwellers.

He placed his ax in the left pocket of his mackinaw and buttoned the flap over the head, the helve sticking out awkwardly, for he had no belt. Easing himself down from the chopping-log, with infinite patience he began the long and painful journey over the crusted snow. Dave prayed that the trap might contain a living thing with which he could still the torment within him, for he knew that without food he could not much longer repel the icy cold. It smote him now more cruelly than

before as he moved out of the faint warmth
that remained in the burnt area, for his energy
had lowered appreciably in the interval, what
with the lengthening fast and the sapping pain
of his leg.

Foot by foot he progressed over the hard
white layer, his arms drawing and his good leg
pushing, the injured member trailing after,
abnormally sensitive to the slightest jar or
strain. With his weight spread as it was the
crust sustained him for long stretches; then
at some weak spot protected from the freezing
wind he would break through and sink down
into the powdery mass beneath. On such occasions he was forced to employ the utmost
caution to regain the harder surface, which
had a tendency to crumble as he advanced upon
it. And only by clamping his jaws hard and
pitting his will against the shrinking of the
flesh could he drag himself out, for the stabbing pain of his leg at these exertions almost
sickened him. His body—his brain too—cried
out for the seductive warmth of the snow
covert, where, if he succumbed to its lure, he

knew he would drowse deliciously into an un-
waking sleep; but always some inner strength
prevailed against the temptation.

Plans for what would follow the journey to
the trap were formulating in his brain as he
crept on his way. Whether or not he found
meat, he would retrace his path and seek refuge
in an immense hollow tree that ages before
had fallen and lay but a few paces distant
from the camp site. Here he could find shelter
from the wind that would rise again with
the going down of the sun, and have a fair
chance to survive the night; and Gabe on his
return would instantly pick up his trail and
search him out. He could go without water
for a long period if need be, and in extremity
would dare the live snow. Food was his consuming thought, and as he neared the end of
his journey he visioned hungrily the catch of
the trap, its quarry in his mind's eye taking
successively the guise of all the woodla1 1
creatures he knew.

He was dimly aware that his thoughts were
wandering. Suddenly full realization of this

came to him and his mind awoke sharply. As it did so he had a queer feeling that some mysterious influence, some occult force lying outside the range of his own powers, had been responsible for the quick clearing of his brain. Then the peculiar intuitive belief that he was the focus of malignant eyes possessed him, and the hairs of his cheeks and around the base of his head prickled at the roots—the reflex of that strange faculty of sensing the stare of unseen hostile orbs, an ancestral gift familiar to all hunters who themselves have been hunted. He held himself rigid and peered about uneasily, searching with keen gaze the thickets of spruce and juniper. But he could discover nothing; even the harmless, companionable dwellers of the trees had vanished, which alone portended an evil presence.

He had all but crested the rise of a low hummock beyond which lay the trap, and he flattened himself to the snow surface and pondered. If he was being stalked by some crafty animal, possibly a panther driven down from the uplands by winter starvation, or a surly old bear that had failed to "hole-up," emboldened by hunger to attack him, his chances were indeed slim. But after a few moments of movelessness, which brought nothing into view, he felt reassured. It suddenly occurred to him that an animal held in the trap, too recently caught to have frozen to death, perhaps had glimpsed his fur cap over the summit and caught his scent, and its glare of implacable hatred at the supposed human cause of its seizure had given rise to the weird sensation.

With this thought he lifted his head slowly and gazed over the crown of the knoll—straight into the brass-yellow, malevolent eyes of a full-grown Canada lynx that crouched over the trap, one immense padded foot on the half-eaten remains of a marten whose leg was held by the steel jaws.

Arrant coward and sneak though he is, the despised "lucivee" of the Northern country can prove a dangerous adversary on occasion. He will fight fiercely when cornered and will sometimes attack man while ravenous with hunger or when knowing him to be helpless; and a

A full-grown Canadian lynx crouched over the trap

maimed man disturbing him at his kill in time of famine cold might well dread the encounter. With tufted ears laid flat back, and teeth bared in a snarl of unbridled savagery, the lynx confronted Dave with the base courage of its tribe when instinctively aware that the human foe is disabled.

The brutal irony of his quest almost overpowered the woodsman's courage. After an unbelievably desperate effort he had found, instead of meat to bring new life into his veins, a ruthless enemy from which he could hardly hope to escape in his weakened, crippled state. A mad impulse to yell, partly in an attempt to cow the animal, partly in the hope that Gabe might be on his trail within ear-shot, was suppressed as the fear came to him that the lynx would be quick to detect the weak quality of his voice and gain courage therefrom; for he was beyond the point where he could command his vocal powers.

As the lynx crouched lower and the spitting and snarling subsided, Dave's practised eye recognized its intent. It had assumed a seem-

185

ingly idiotic posture, like that of a fawning dog, its fore-body hugging the snow, its hinder part grotesquely raised; a pose due to the disproportionate length of the rabbit-like hind legs, superbly fashioned for immense springing power.

The big cat's rump rocked slightly from side to side, coördinating all its whip-cord sinews for the spring. Dave sensed that the crucial moment had come. He already had reached to his pocket and secured his ax. Swiftly he drew it back over his shoulder, and with all the strength his will could summon hurled it at the creature's head.

At close quarters the small, straight-handled ax in skilled hands is a weapon of marvelous efficiency, and used as a missile is as deadly as an Indian's tomahawk. In its varied uses Dave had the expertness of the trained woodsman; but a sick rage flamed in his heart the instant the ax left his hand. For the frost coating of his mitten had caused the smooth haft to slip prematurely from his grip; and instead of flying true it shot upward.

THE SURVIVAL

But Dave's dismay was short-lived. The lynx had leaped a fractional part of a second before the ax slipped, rising high to clear the distance; and by a miracle meeting the razor-keen blade in mid-air, its skull was cleft cleanly between the eyes, and it thudded to the snow, a writhing heap of ash-tawny fur, almost within reach of the trapper's hand.

Dave's grunt of relief at the outcome was mingled with astonishment. An infinitesimal part of a second's divergence in the action of man or beast would have meant for him only a few minutes of life, ghastly with the work of envenomed teeth and claws. His mis-throw had been most opportune, for the impact of the ax was more than doubled by the opposing force of the hurtling body; and Dave took heart at this evidence that luck was with him.

The stricken eyes of the lynx still glared at the man with a tameless ferocity, which held him with its uncanny fascination until death filmed them. The convulsive movements of the body were soon stilled, and Dave drew himself closer and retrieved his weapon. Here

187

was meat, tough and stringy and raw, but warm and life-sustaining. He resolutely overcame his repugnance and employed the ax to obtain a chunk of the flesh, with which he proceeded to satisfy his craving.

The hot, reeking lump was almost unchewable, but it infused new vitality into his jaded body, and after partaking of all that his stomach would stand, he turned about and began the torturous, floundering journey back. The day was now well advanced and Dave hastened his awkward movements, unmindful of the pain they brought, that he might reach shelter before darkness.

"I jest got to git there," he muttered doggedly as he brought his racked and tired frame into swifter action. "'Tain't but a little distance, now, to the old windfall, an' I'll make it, I reckon, if my arms hold out," he encouraged himself, and set his teeth upon the resolution.

He continued to mutter thickly in approaching delirium as night drew on and he neared the spot where the cabin had stood. The wind already was rising. Soon it blew bitingly through the forest lanes, its cruel blasts laden with the chill of broad Arctic reaches, and it spurred the crawling trapper to still greater effort.

As he approached the clearing Dave swerved to the left and sought the snow-choked mouth of the hollow tree that was to be his haven until help arrived. Reaching it, he dug weakly at the opening until he could gain entrance, and laboriously drew himself into the cavity with his last remaining strength. He was dizzy and breathless with the exertion and lay huddled for a moment while he fought to regain his grip on himself.

The hollow was unexpectedly warm and filled with a pungent, musty odor which puzzled him for an instant. Suddenly recognition of the smell came to him, and was attested by a movement as of some bulky animal and a menacing growl. As his searching eyes, becoming accustomed to the gloom, glimpsed dimly a large furry form, the shock of his discovery sent the blood from his brain, and his senses reeled. Weak, anguished with pain, and overcome by this crowning horror of the day, the woodsman's resolute will broke, and he fainted. As consciousness left him there floated in his vision a pair of fierce eyes and savagely grinning jaws, and his last thought was of the fury of a hibernating bear disturbed in its winter sleep.

Gabe Shaddick, having been delayed in leaving Little Gap owing to the day's absence of the trader, started back twenty-four hours late. He covered the miles between the post and a certain familiar sheltered spot at his best speed, the rhythmic swing of his snowshoes continuing hour after hour untiringly, for the going was perfect. Reaching this half-way point just before sundown, he threw off his pack and removed his snowshoes at the base of a low overhanging cliff where the setting of his night's camp on the way in remained undisturbed. Hurriedly making a fire, he fried a thick slice of salt pork and brewed some tea. After consuming these he added a few balsam boughs to the heap in the bottom of the scooped-out hole in the snow, smoked his pipe, and, building up his fire, rolled himself up in his blankets for three hours' sleep. He was anxious to get back, for the long line of traps needed the constant attention of two men; the catch was likely to be eaten by prowlers if not removed quickly.

At nine o'clock Gabe awoke, fully restored during his short sleep by the vivifying ozone of the forest. He made and drank another huge draught of tea, secured the snowshoes to his feet, slung the pack on his back, and set out over the trail for the cabin. The moon was up and shed its clear brilliance over the white-gleaming surface, crisscrossed with the black shadows of the forest growth. As the night advanced the moon went down, but Gabe suffered no interruption to his steady stride. The hard glitter of the stars, that seemed to twinkle into life by the million as the moon set, diffused a radiance that made the trail an open road to the woodsman's eyes; and Gabe concluded that he could make the camp by sunup.

The streaming pennons of rosy dawn were quivering across the snow-blanketed world as Gabe approached the clearing. He wondered at the absence of smoke from the cabin stove, which should have been twisting through the high branches at this hour of the morning, and surmised that Dave had been overtaken by night on the line and had camped at the cache. As he pierced the tree-tops with enquiring eyes, something in the appearance of the sky-line puzzled him. Suddenly it was borne in upon him that the crest of the giant pine was missing. Perturbed, he strode forward with increased speed, and in a few minutes burst upon the desolate scene that awaited him.

The main points of the drama he grasped in an instant. Circling the burned spot, his progress made difficult by the prostrate pine, he scanned the snow anxiously for indications of his partner's escape from the ruin. Quickly he found the trail and in it read more of the story. Unloosing his pack, he sent forth a loud, carrying cry that boomed and echoed through the tree-studded spaces but brought no reply. Whereupon he started off along the well-defined track, and had followed it for only a few paces when he came to where Dave had branched off on his return journey. Swerving to this newer path, he ran it down to the mouth of the old windfall, across the center of which lay the branching top of the pine.

Kicking off his snowshoes, Gabe cleared away the snow that the wind had lodged about the opening and crawled inside the great hollow log. In the dim light he made out his partner's feet. Calling him by name, but getting no response, he advanced as far as the cramped space would permit, and was dumfounded when a savage, throaty snarl, sounding alarmingly close in the narrow confines, assailed his ears. A quick impulse to back out was as quickly overcome. His eyes, now adjusted to the semi-darkness, peered into the recesses of the hollow and made out the form of the bear, struggling and growling threateningly, but strangely indisposed, or unable, to advance. He could not fathom this, but apparently there was no immediate danger of an onslaught.

Gabe ran his hand inside Dave's shirt and felt a faint stirring. Overjoyed at this evidence that the spark remained, he withdrew from the log and with infinite patience and gentleness, having noted the rudely bandaged leg, got his partner out of the cavity and began roughly to chafe and slap his cheeks. The senseless man stirred and muttered protestingly, and at this Gabe sprang to his feet. At a little distance he scooped a long, wide trough in the snow with a snowshoe and lined a section of the bottom deeply with spruce tips. Carefully lifting his partner upon this soft, sheltered bed, he built a fire at one end, and then ran back for his pack.

Soon hot mouthfuls of strong and bitter tea, brewed in a pannikin over the fire, brought the rescued man to his senses. This was followed by a thick gruel of pounded parched corn, administered by Gabe in small doses. And then, with strength visibly returning, Dave sketched briefly the ordeal of the previous day.

THE SURVIVAL

When he reached the point of his invasion of the winter quarters of a bear he stopped, puzzled over his immunity from attack.

Gabe, puzzled himself, got up and strode over to the ancient fallen monarch, doubtless a remote ancestor of the kingly pine whose head was now bowed down upon it. Closely he examined the spot where the broken branches lay in a tangled mass over the decaying shell. Chuckling at his discovery he returned to his partner.

"We ain't been neighborly," he remarked with tantalizing irrelevance, backwoods etiquette requiring that his deep feeling of relief over Dave's preservation be carefully concealed by a bantering manner. "Here we been livin' right next door to a bear, an' we ain't never called—not till you happened in last night an' went to sleep in his front parlor. How do you reckon two old trap-men like us overlooked a bear den right under our noses?"

"Well, he likely holed up afore we come," suggested Dave impatiently, "an' it snowed an' covered up his lodgin's so 's we did n't see nothin' unusual about the old blow-down. Consarn ye, Gabe, why don't ye tell me why he did n't chaw me up?"

"Guess you was n't lucky, you old timber rat!" Gabe began his explanation. "One o' those big straight limbs o' that cussed pine broke off in the middle when it hit the ground, and the crown bounced up and drove the sharp end plumb through the old windfall. That 's the way I figger it. It must 've pinned that sleepin' bear tight up against the side o' the holler, so 's he could n't git at you; but gosh! I bet it did wake him up sudden like! Least-ways, we got a prime bear pelt out o' the rumpus."

Dave glowered at him. "No, we hain't, not by a jugful," he protested with spirit. "That there old cuss kep' me from freezin' to death, and we 're a-goin' to pry out that limb and give him a chance to skedaddle out o' here. that 's what!"

"Well, mebbe you 're right," responded his partner, with an indulgent grin. "It *would*

196

be a low-down trick, I reckon, to spile sech a good heatin' stove, 'specially since the old base-burner did n't have you hoppin' up all night to keep it goin'!"

THE REFUGEE

THE REFUGEE

THE puma stiffened into an attitude of strained inquiry as an unfamiliar, disquieting odor came to her nostrils. The puzzling scent scattered all thought of her mission, which was to seek a lick where a salt-hungry deer might reasonably be expected to reward her stalk. As she stood sniffing curiously, a deer came bounding down an aisle of the forest, eyes wide with a fear that was not of the red-tawny, dangerous beast in its path. Hardly swerving from the direct line of its flight, the deer passed the still wondering cat at so close a margin that its hereditary enemy involuntarily shrunk aside to escape the flying, sharp-edged hoofs. The puma growled low in her throat, swaying her head from side to side up the wind in an endeavor to sift the strange smell and determine its meaning. More deer came hurtling by, each presenting opportunity for a back-breaking spring or a buffet at close quarters from the puma's sickle-armed paws, but as unmindful as she of the offered chance. This astounding contempt of her presence bewildered her as much as the unknown smell. Never before in her experience had she known so utter a disregard of her arrogant self.

A wildly snorting moose bull came charging down through the trees, muffled nose outstretched, antlers laid back on the maned hump of his shoulders; and was shortly followed by others of his family, cows and calves racing by with but scant thought of family ties. Then a legion of the forest wildings began to pass, rabbits negligent of the snakelike streaking of a weasel through their ranks, foxes running belly to earth with tails drooping, a wolf no longer the implacable foe of all living things; and in the air arose a terror-stricken beating of wings as blue jays, owls, butcher-birds—a medley of the winged life of the forest—winnowed through the upper spaces of the wood.

A wildly snorting moose bull came charging down through
the trees

THE REFUGEE

The terrifying odor grew stronger, and some new quality in it began to smart the sensitive membranes of nose and throat and eyes. A strangling haze settled upon the atmosphere and it became increasingly difficult to breathe in sufficient air to keep the lungs up to their work of supplementing the mad straining of muscles. A faint moaning sound that had arisen swelled gradually until it became a roar interspersed with the sharp crackling of smitten wood, driving the animals to greater speed over the uneven floor of the forest.

The fear of the mad company was communicated to the puma, but the impulse to turn tail and flee with it was for a brief time overcome by a vague loneliness for her mate. He had left her, to hunt alone, and her eyes now eagerly sought him among the myriad life that was flowing past. She whined anxiously, then lifted her voice in a screaming summons. A minute passed without reply, and her courage oozed. Whirling about in sudden panic, she joined the hurrying throng.

While the puma was hesitating the forest

fire had approached at terrific speed under the urge of a north wind, and its flaming guidons were now flanking the frantic four-footed rabble. Retarded at the center by the wet spread of a marsh, the wings had advanced with undiminished speed. They soon would join in front, and only the faintest chance of evading the encircling wall of fire was offered the panicky mob of which the puma was now a member. The flames were rapidly drawing closer on all sides, save for a small clear space ahead toward which the animals converged in a turbulent stream. The smaller among them were crushed under the feet of the more powerful, and shrill screams came from the unfortunate beasts that were stricken and left to the ravening element. Overhead writhing yellow tongues licked at the topmost branches of the trees, and fiery brands fell in a shower on the surging, living tide. Dense, pungent smoke began to swirl in choking clouds throughout the ranks, which were thinning appreciably as the animals were overwhelmed by one or another of the odds against them.

THE REFUGEE

Now in the forefront of the mob, a position which she had attained by her great leaping ability, the puma strained her muscles in an effort to reach the gap in the tightening circle of flame. Her cat's sense warned her that she could not long sustain this speed, and all the power of her tough, corded sinews was exerted to drive the sleek body toward the opening before they lost their first strength. By a tremendous spurt she reached the narrow outlet and passed the line of fire, tongue hanging from black-rimmed lips and lungs near to bursting with the effort and the scorching air. Only a pitiful remnant of the horde were as fortunate, none but the fleet and strong among the multitude winning through. The rest remained to shrivel in the vast oven into which their forest sanctuary had been converted, perhaps by some heedless camper whose fire had been left to smolder and burn deep into the tinderlike humus, eventually to burst into living, devastating flame.

The puma's instinct, as that of the other fortunates, drew her to a watercourse in the cleft of a range of low stony hills that lay to the south; and thither the small army of outcasts directed their way at such speed of which they were capable. Exhausted by the first terrific effort, their muscles were now reacting solely to the stimulus of terror, and once the keen edge of that was gone they were content to plunge into the chill waters of a wide pool of the stream and there stay until a closer approach of the fire willed otherwise.

But the puma was not of a mind to remain here longer than to lap up a cooling drink. She had the cat tribe's aversion to wetting her fur, and the depths of the pool offered her no alluring haven. Also she was swayed by a mad desire to forsake the haunts that had been so rudely invaded by a strange, consuming enemy that she could not hope to combat, and which of a certainty had devoured her mate. She was still fearful of the flames that could yet be heard, but which were advancing less rapidly because they must climb the rocky rampart that bordered the stream; and the lure of distant woods where the scorching winds could not follow drew her from the temporary refuge.

Her muzzle still dripping with the cool draught, the puma sprang from her crouching position at the pool's edge and raced downstream along the bank. Her steady progress —no longer a series of leaps but a smooth, sinuous run—carried her on at fair speed. Where the low banks offered a path away from the water she glided snakelike through the brush, and when high cliffs guarded the narrowed stream she bounded along the boulder-strewn edge of the torrent with the sure-footedness of her kind. Here and there along the way she snapped up an unwary rabbit or a grouse huddled beneath a low-limbed spruce; but seldom did she pause for more than a few brief minutes in her race from the accursed enemy that had sought to shrivel her into lifelessness with its hot breath.

The fire had been left far behind by now; it had, as a matter of fact, swerved to the eastward under the influence of a changing wind, and the puma had long since placed herself be-

yond its reach.   But she had not yet come to a
land where she felt that her safety was as-
sured, and through the night and far into the
next day she continued her flight along the
widening current of the Swiftwater.   But her
pace now was languishing with the strain of
her unwonted effort, for in common with her
kin she was not of an inclination for travel;
and only the spur of her recent terror kept her
to her quest.

Toward mid-afternoon of the second day
the puma came to a gorge out of which the
stream swung in an abrupt curve, and as she
neared the limits of the upthrust of rock at the
point of the bend, she slowed down and cautiously approached the opening.   There was
no telling what might lie beyond that sudden
turn.   As she peered around the granite wall
her eyes fell on a gleaming silver sheet fringed
with low grass-grown shores, beyond which
rose a forest of dark-green spruce, a fairy spot
where the stream lost its turbulence to feed a
quiet backwater.   Here was a restful, safe-
appearing haven that invited her tired body.

No suffocating, searing flame could invade that rock-girt intervale, where for the first time since the beginning of her flight she felt secure.

As she emerged into the open, she dropped suddenly into a tense, crouching pose. Her roving gaze had fallen on a smooth brown patch half shielded by a growth of shrubs that sprang from the water's farther edge. So much like her own sleek hide was it in color and texture that her alert senses recognized it at once as the flank of a deer; and the enticing prospect revived her flagging spirits. The inlet was so sheltered from the wind that neither animal had scented the other, and the puma skirted the margin of the pool toward the unsuspecting deer in a lithe, snaky crawl. No whisper of her coming reached the object of her stalk, a fat doe that had stepped out of the cool woods with her half-grown fawn to bask for a fleeting moment in the sunlight that poured over the water-meadow in a golden haze. At a little distance the fawn lay on a dry, mossy knoll behind a screen of "Indian tea" which concealed it from the intruder's eyes.

The puma's stealthy advance brought her within a few rods of her intended quarry. She gathered herself into a compact mass of tautened muscle, her long tail twitching nervously, and bounded swiftly and almost noiselessly forward. At the second leap the doe awoke to her peril. She snorted a warning to her offspring and quivered into sudden action; but too late. The big cat was upon her as she whirled about, with barbed paws gripping her back and flanks and strong, sharp teeth tearing at her neck. Her back was broken and the jugular severed almost instantly in the mad onslaught of claws and fangs, and she sank lifeless under her savage assailant.

The eyes of the puma, glowing with green fire in the ecstasy of killing, took note of the escaping fawn, and tempted by the awakened lust of the hunt she sprang from the body of the doe to intercept it. But the nimble little fugitive showed so swift a set of heels that she changed her mind and returned to her kill.

THE REFUGEE

She dragged the carcass a little way into the wood and feasted on venison until the drowsy comfort of satiation overcame her gluttony. Then she scratched a covering of leaves and brush over what remained of the meat, and seeking a spruce thicket near by, coiled her satisfied body on the soft earth, and slept.

The fire-driven fugitive's seeking was at an end. Here in this bounteous region where good hunting and security were promised she was content to make her new home. The rocky eminence offered safe retreat from any danger that might threaten, and the rolling woodland surely harbored much game, as she already had reason to be aware.

Following a long sleep during which she digested the enormous meal of venison and restored her spent tissues after the long-drawn effort of her flight, she ate again of the deer, hid the remnant as before, and trotted off to explore her surroundings. A fissure high up in the face of the cliff led to a wide cavity within the rock, and here she determined to make her lair. The rock-split was barely accessible, the way to it lying along a narrow broken shelf over which she had to scramble with all her cat's agility; and at the end of the path a leap of fully fifteen feet, up and across a cleft in the mass, was necessary to reach the portal. Once past it, she was safe from all intrusion; only her own kind, and the eagles, could attain this high, stone-buttressed domicile.

This excellent dwelling-place she discovered toward the close of the day. After springing into the fissure and investigating its interior, she returned to the shelf from which her leap was made for a last careful inspection of her dooryard. Below her on one side spread the shallow backwater of the stream, rippleless in the calm of evening, a blue gem rimmed with a crescent of meadow richly tinted with the russet and gold of autumn. At its distant brim the sear grasses and shrubs gave way to sturdier growth in a gloomy curving wall of forest. Early dusk already had fallen upon the glade, whence the vespers of piping frogs and nocturnal insects arose faintly to the puma's unheeding ears. The last rays of the sun washed the rough face of the cliff with splashes of glinting copper, and made of the tawny sentinel figure a gleaming bronze statue as the big cat stood motionless for an instant and gazed unblinkingly into the dully glowing orb.

She turned her head and swept keen eyes over the black-green forest roof that spread below her eyrie, but nothing met her vision that was not eloquent of solitude and safety. Her vague forebodings that she might have trespassed upon the domain of beasts more powerful than herself were quieted by her survey with eye and ear, and she suddenly wheeled and sprang for the threshold of the cave. Well satisfied with her new realm, over which she doubtless could maintain the same sway that she and her mate had exercised over the old range to the north, the puma established herself for the night.

But the invader from the North country would have felt less confident had she known that beyond the southern edge of the forest, where the wild stream merged with another and formed a wider and statelier stream, lay a settlement where dwelt the dread man creatures who had an unending dispute with her kind for dominance over the wilds. No knowledge of that disquieting fact disturbed her rest, and she came forth in the dawn of the morning arrogant in her power over all the inhabitants of this most promising field.

During the days that followed her advent upon the backwater she traveled over the country in a constantly widening circle. When the deer had been consumed she found the hunting as good as her initial experience promised, for the forest folk at first fell an easy prey to this new and unfamiliar menace, and with the plenitude of meat she would have waxed fat and slothful had her habit not been of a nervous, never-ending activity. By turns she prowled the ragged heights of her granite citadel and quested the low-lying regions of marsh and meadow and spruce woods watered by the stream that had guided her to these alluring pastures.

But the wildings of the neighborhood—
those that survived a first acquaintance with
her—soon came to know of the presence of the
stealthy, quick-leaping terror, and to their
habitual caution was added a vigilance that
gradually brought necessity for the sharpen-
ing of her wits and a widening of her hunting-
zone, if she would keep her belly full. So
that her sleek sides were not burdened of fat
and the luster of her pale fox-red coat was
not dimmed by a life of luxury and ease. But
game of one kind or another was plentiful
enough for her needs, and sufficient meat fell
to her prowess to make her content with this
hopitable wilderness, where nothing happened
to disturb her serenity save the longing for her
mate that came to her at times. On these occasions—usually when a cold, pallid moon rode
high in the sky—she would scream in mournful
protest against her loneliness; but only the
startled, sleepy birds made answer.

As time passed, the growing wariness of the
deer of the region, which were becoming familiar with her methods, with increasing fre-

quency brought failure to her attempts to secure a meal of venison. Often when she got within leaping-distance of a feeding buck or doe, the alert animal would sense her presence and bound into safety, its white flag flaunted insolently in her face. Yet many a gashed and crimsoned flank bore evidence of the fractional margin by which its owner had escaped the clutch of her ripping claws. Gradually she was forced to depend mainly on hares and grouse and other smaller folk of the wilderness for her food, which diet was varied only at lengthening intervals by venison when good fortune attended her deer-stalking.

One day as she was about to drink, stretched flat on a fallen tree that slanted down into the stream where it quieted at the entrance to the backwater, her face almost touching the surface so that the depths were clearly revealed, a large and languorous trout swept slowly up into her vision, passing only a few inches below the quick-seeing eyes. The instinct to strike at any living thing within her reach caused the puma to dart a lightning-swift paw at the unsuspecting swimmer, and the scooping sweep of her clawed foot threw it far up on the bank. A quick, doubling leap from her position brought her upon the prize before it could more than give one convulsive flop in the dry grass; and its brilliant spotted beauty faded before her appetite in a few hurried gulps.

The puma licked her lips appreciatively over the pink-fleshed morsel. Here was new and delicious fare, to be obtained by the easiest method known to her experience. She had eaten fish on rare occasions in the past, but they had been coarse-fibered suckers or others of sluggish habit, cast up on the shore dead or dying, or stranded in some depression by a sudden lowering of the waters. These had been vastly different provender from the sweet and firm meat of the trout.

She returned to the partly submerged windfall, confident of her ability to secure a satisfying meal of this new delicacy. But though she lay crouched and expectant on the log until her muscles stiffened, she was not again rewarded. At length she abandoned the attempt and withdrew to ravage the thickets for furred or feathered game with which to appease her hunger. She did not, however, forget the delectable flavor of the fish, and her occasional renewed endeavors to draw a trout from the cool waters of the stream were sometimes successful, so that this new mode of hunting became a part of her curriculum. But with the passing of the days the icy winds that came whistling down from the wide Arctic snow-fields locked the waters against her further inroads, and she could no longer vary her diet with fish.

In the course of time, the puma's farings carried her to the southern limits of the spruce woods. One midday in early autumn, when an unwonted dampness in the air carried scents to a great distance, she detected an unfamiliar but subtly fascinating odor that was wafted to her nostrils from down the stream. She followed the enticing smell, and shortly came to a sweep of curious woodland where to her forest-bred understanding the tree-boles seemed to have stopped growing a little above the ground, and were here and there smothered with dense, leafless brush.

The belt of wild pasture-land to which she had come was a hilly expanse of rocks and raw stumps and brush, a half-conquered region bordering the tilled acres of the settlement— that middle ground where farm clearings merge gradually into the ancient forest from which they had been hewed. Dotting this area were several strange beasts that appeared to the puma to bear a faint resemblance to the deer of her experience, or perhaps they more nearly resembled the less familiar moose. They were browsing on the scanty herbage with a lack of vigilance that the puma could not understand, and did not seem at all disturbed by the harsh jangling sound arising from their midst that was very disquieting to her own wary senses.

The smell of them at close range both repelled and attracted her. It had a new, confusing quality that moved her to study this peculiar game long and craftily. She ranged the edge of the pasture where it met the wood, eying the cattle with contempt for their apparent stupidity, and yet half fearful of attacking them. At length a whiff of her own pungent odor drew the attention of an old bull, and he turned toward the wall of trees and snorted angrily. The rest of the scattered herd, heeding the note of warning, lifted their heads and gazed with mildly curious eyes in the same direction. Abruptly they rushed into close formation, tossing their horns defiantly as the puma came gliding out of her concealment, voracity having conquered her fear. The jangling sound that had been the chief cause of her indecision she discovered came from one animal; it seemed to emanate from a strange growth at the neck, and her awe of it lessened somewhat with the locating of its source.

Suddenly the cattle with one accord wheeled and fled in panic across the pasture, their slow bovine senses at last awakening to the menace of this threatening, slinking intruder. The puma needed only the evidence of their dread to harden her courage. A few swift bounds and she was within leaping-distance of the rearmost member, a yearling Hereford bull. She sprang upon his back, and clinging with deep-set claws to the terrified animal sought the veins of his neck with practised teeth. He stumbled on gamely for a distance, his mad snorts finally ending in a plaintive, gurgling sigh as he sank to the ground; and the puma, after gazing distrustfully toward the cleared land that had now come into view, fell to a warm satisfying meal of young beef.

When she had eaten her fill she fled back to her lair in the rock tower by the backwater, too suspicious of danger that might lurk in so open a space to remain in the vicinity of her kill until it was devoured. But the next morning she returned to the carcass for another meal. As she approached it the repellent odor arising from many strange tracks that surrounded the body stiffened her into an attitude of half angry alarm. She sniffed distrustfully at the footprints, then turned and streaked for the woods, prudence overcoming her desire for a second gorging.

The puma had fortuitously escaped an acquaintance with man, up in the old wilderness domain from which the fire had driven her; but she had come upon his works on several occasions and she knew the hated man odor, which the wild kindred are early taught is a portent of danger; and she had no desire to try conclusions with him, though she bared her fangs in sullen anger over his interference with her kill.

But she could not withstand the lure of this rich hunting-ground and she made frequent excursions to the pastures fringing the settlement. The caution awakened in her by a subtle understanding that day was man's time for ranging led her to pursue her explorations chiefly by night. Under cover of the protecting darkness, which to her cat's eyes was no more than a dusky haze, she drew closer in to the farmsteads and soon was levying tribute on the settlers' live-stock. She learned that certain tasty fowls, occasional truants from the barnyard, roosted in trees at the pasture's lower edge, and these she found easy to search out and claw from their perches. Once she mustered courage to approach a pig-pen, whence issued a most seductive aroma, but the shrill squealing from within that arose when she sniffed and scratched at the board walls, and the echoing alarm of an aroused dog, drove her fearsomely from the neighborhood.

The sheepfolds in the course of time engaged her attention. She had discovered a small flock one night, huddled in the angle of a fence, and marveling at the cowardice of these shrinking, thick-furred beasts that made no slightest effort to fight back, she struck right and left at the cowering white forms and killed with the pure lust of slaughter. She gorged herself upon warm blood that night, and finally slunk back into the woods a convert to the rare delight of sheep-killing. She did not again find the flock in the open, but eventually trailed it to an enclosure which she entered without great difficulty; and several times thereafter she gratified her acquired appetite for mutton.

The puma had conquered the border-land as

she had conquered the forest, and her arrogance grew with the victory. Of man she still knew nothing through sight or actual contact; he still existed to her merely as an odor of hereditary abhorrence, an unseen, threatening presence whose works, redolent of his touch, bestrewed her new land of conquest. Her intuition told her that the strange species of game that fell so easily to her attack were somehow under man's protection, and she lived in instinctive apprehension of his reprisals for her toll upon them. Wholly catlike in the quality of her wits, she was able through craft and uncanny prescience to evade the crude traps and ambuscades arranged for her undoing, and her slight endowment of courage was in consequence seldom put to the test.

But for all the puma tribe's ancestral awe of man, there come occasions in the lives of these big cats when some inexplicable reversal of their nature brings forgetfulness of fear. And one day in late October, when a youth in soundless moccasins crossed the fields and loomed suddenly before her eyes as she lay dozing in a tangle of brush, the apparition brought no panic to her, but rather a freakish desire to play with the harmless-appearing intruder. Perhaps a stomach full to repletion robbed her alike of dread and savagery; possibly a spasm of loneliness for her mate led her to seek sympathy from the first animate thing that crossed her vision; or it may have been an overweening desire to torment, as a cat a mouse, this life that she sensed was in her power. Howbeit, she sprang from her concealment and pounced lightly upon the astounded lad, who was bowled over by the impact. She leaped back and sprang again, without a trace of ill nature, and the terrified boy, too weak with fright to use his voice, was mauled about by the padded paws in an ecstasy of feline enjoyment.

Then for an instant the puma stood over him, mouth open with her exertions, apparently studying this remarkable creature whom, heretofore unseen, she had held in such distrust, and who seemed so inoffensive in the flesh. The lad flung his hand up quickly to shield himself from those horrid ivory fangs that seemed to be about to sink into his throat, and in so doing rasped his knuckles against her sharp incisors. A deep scratch resulted and the slight blood exudation smeared her lips. She licked at it—and suddenly all her dormant ferocity flamed into life, the playful spirit swept away by the aroused blood lust. With ears laid back and eyes closed to slits she snarled savagely through bared teeth and crouched on the body, her now unsheathed claws pinning it down and twitching with desire to rend. In another moment her murderous weapons would have done their work, when a providential interruption occurred.

A disquieting sound had come to the puma's ears, and it brought her into a quick, questioning pause as she sought its origin. The sight her eyes fell upon caused her to spring from the prostrate form and slink away under cover of the stone fence, then leap it and streak for the woods in abject fear. As the tawny shape

curved into the air the man driving a span of
oxen that were snaking a big fire-log across
the clearing greeted the vision with a piercing
yell such as the dismayed puma had never
heard. Her dim reasoning conceived it as a
despairing cry of the human, which assuredly the monster had in its clutches! While
the man himself was ignored, the terrible
sound added speed to the fugitive's flight, and
she shot over the open and darted into the
gloom of the trees balked of her human prey
by the most puzzling menace she had ever
known.

Had the two persons concerned in this adventure been aware of its true effect upon the
puma they would have had less cause for gloating over her discomfiture. For she had tasted
man's blood and the awakened lust for it would
not die; she had worsted a human in the easiest
encounter of her life, and found him almost
non-resistent—a poor foeman whom she would
always afterward hold in half-contempt.
Henceforth man was to be numbered among
her victims.

To the folk of the settlement this last outrage of the alien from the North country came as the crowning injury of a long series. It was viewed, of course, as a savage attack, inspired only by desire to kill. From the first indication of its presence the tracks it left told the older among them that the visitor was a panther, by which name the puma is generally known, though it is called also cougar, catamount, and mountain-lion; and occasionally the more popular name is corrupted to "painter." For years no panther had been known to visit the vicinity of this far outpost of civilization, the original dwellers having long since been killed off or sought a wilderness more remote from man. The men of the village expected confidently to put an end to the interloper in short order, but their efforts were unsuccessful, either through mere ill luck or because an intelligence superior to that of most of her kind enabled the big cat to escape traps and hunters alike. In fact none had even obtained a glimpse of her, until she indulged her whimsical impulse to play with one of them.

THE REFUGEE

Her depredations, that in spite of all precautions grew more frequent as time passed, began to assume a serious aspect. The inroads upon the meager flocks of the little backwoods farms became a menace to the comfort and well-being of the owners, for the margin between want and enough for needs is slight in these isolated communities on the borders of the upper fur country. The men who followed trapping for a livelihood during the season, and who were best able to cope with such a problem, were absent on their grounds far to the north, preparing for the winter fur-taking; and those who remained wore out their wits in a fruitless endeavor to trap or hunt down the wary beast. Her tracks they had often followed, but never to the quiet backwater of which she was the guardian; for the way to her rock castle passed for a considerable distance over a dry, boulder-covered stream-bed from which the Swiftwater had been deflected ages before by some upheaval of nature. Here her trail was always lost, and none had been able to pick it up again at the point of emergence. The few nondescript dogs of the village could not be persuaded to follow the scent beyond the edge of the pasture; the panther smell was not to their liking, for most of them had encountered the animal on nocturnal occasions without profit to themselves. So the people of the village were in a state of growing uneasiness as to how much of their live-stock would be left to carry them through the winter.

That the panther would attack a human being was doubted by the older men, for there were few instances known of such occurrences, these being only at times of great hunger; and heaven knew that the stealthy marauder was not famishing for food, as witness its all-too-frequent banquets almost before their very doors! But there were those among the settlement folk, principally women and children, who lived in terror of the invader. Now and again its blood-chilling screech could be heard on still, moonlit nights when it called lonesomely for the mate that would not come; and the unearthly cry as of a soul in torment hardened the belief of the more timid in its fierceness. Then came the long-expected assault upon one of their number which threw them into a panic of fear.

Young Jamie MacGowan, whom the panther had sprung upon as he was crossing the fields, was brought back to the village in a state of collapse, by Pete Duncan, who had providentially appeared on the scene with his ox team.

"Lucky me and the oxen happened along when we did," explained Pete, while Jamie was collecting his faculties. An excited throng had gathered by the blacksmith's forge, where the pair halted to tell of the assault. " 'T was a monstrous big cat, about ten feet long, I reckon, and it had the lad down and was jest a-goin' to tear him to pieces. Me and old Bright an' Brindle scairt it off, and it cut lively fer the woods, I tell ye! Sure ye 're all sound, Jamie?"

Jamie shivered and nodded. He was not far from hysterical tears, but gradually youthful appreciation of being the center of a thrilling encounter drove away his terror. By nightfall he was proudly describing the attack

—it was now a hand-to-claw fight—and reveling in the light that beats upon heroic combat.

"We better borry a pack o' bear-dogs an' track it down," asserted the blacksmith. "Ary one of us, 'specially the women-folks an' youngsters, won't be safe while that varmint runs loose, now it's got started on folks. Let's send over to Roarin' Branch Post fer their hounds an' have a Thanksgivin' cat-hunt."

This suggestion met with instant favor. The smith's helper was dispatched for the pack of mixed hound and bull blood that doubtless would take up the panther's trail with enthusiasm. This was Tuesday. He would get back with the dogs by Wednesday night, and on Thursday, which had been proclaimed Dominion Thanksgiving Day, they would turn out in force and hunt down the murderous, thieving creature.

In the interval there was no evidence of the panther's return to the clearing. A number of the men secretly kept armed watch during a good part of the two nights following; but only the panther's fierce, echoing scream from the

depths of the forest on the second night—
which they chose to accept as either a threat
or a challenge—gave proof that it remained
in the neighborhood. Apparently the scare it
had received had not worn off.

Early on Thanksgiving morning, while the
darkness of the lengthening nights still
shrouded the land, the able-bodied men and
older boys of the settlement, armed with rifles,
set off with the excited pack for the north
pasture. Here they would penetrate the woods
and cast loose the dogs to pick up the trail. It
was the season of frost and snow-flurries that
precedes real winter in these latitudes, and a
sprinkling of snow that covered the ground
promised easy tracking.

When they had been gone for half an hour
or so the alert ears of those who remained behind heard the faint belling of hounds that
betokened the finding of the scent. Whereupon they turned to the preliminaries for late
Thanksgiving dinners, that a rich repast might
await the hoped-for successful return of the
hunters.

In the cottage of Dave MacWhirter, who was far north on his trapping-grounds for the winter, his wife Sally and her sister Margy busied themselves in arrangements for the big feast. The baby rolled about on the rag rug, with gurgling enthusiasm beating the turkey's feet on the floor while they prepared the fat bird for the oven. The elder son Tom was with the hunters, and Dave junior, a lad of ten, denied the privilege of joining the party because of his youth, had gone off with his twenty-two rifle, squirrel-shooting. Savory smells permeated the plain little kitchen sitting-room as the pies baked and the cranberries sputted on the wood-range. Sally MacWhirter, sitting in a wide-armed chair, which she constantly occupied now because of a severe, laming attack of rheumatism, dwelt on the prospects of acquiring a panther-skin rug for the floor.

"I reckon Tommy 'll stand as good a chance as any o' baggin' the critter; he 's the best shot, savin' his pa, in the village."

"Leastways, I hope *somebody* gits a panther

skin to-day; it 'll be a mighty good riddance when that ornery beast 's killed," commented Margy. "I 'm like to jump out o' my own every time I hear an owl screech, my nerves is that upset with the critter's doin's."

"I wish Dave was to home to-day. If he 'd been here he 'd 've fixed it long ago.—What 's that, I wonder!"

A series of shrill yelps came from the yard. Something had aroused the mongrel pup that was outside patiently awaiting the return of its master.

"Look outside, Margy, an' see what ails Buster."

Margy ran to the window. Her face paled as she gazed out, and she stood staring tensely for a second, then turned a stricken look upon her sister, who saw the expression and reached down instinctively for the baby.

"What is it, Margy? Quick—tell me!"

"It 's the panther! Oh, whatever are we to do? He 's clawin' Buster to pieces, an' I reckon he means to come in after us!" Then she steeled herself to her responsibilities, and

turned swiftly toward the wall where the big rifle hung when not in use. Of course it was n't there; Tom had taken it. She quickly came to a decision as to the only thing to do. She recalled hearing of panthers that had entered houses in an excess of boldness, and the cottage was no place for two women and a baby with one of the most bloodthirsty in the annals of the countryside prowling about the yard.

"We 'll have to take the baby an' run out the back door an' over to Lem Doolittle's. We dassent stay here, Sally; we got no way o' killin' the critter or keepin' it out. We can git away afore it sees us. Quick! Let me take the baby." Margy snatched the babe from the mother, who was cuddling it close to still its protests.

"But I can't, Margy, you know I can't!" wailed Sally. "I can't even walk, an' I 'd fall an'—"

"But you must, Sally!" rejoined her sister, fiercely. "I can't leave you, an' we jest got to git out o' here!" The yelps of the valiant little dog ceased, and the women caught the sound of padding claws drawing closer.

"You take the baby an' run, Margy. Help me into the closet an' latch the door, an' I'll be safe. I jest could n't git over to Lem's; I know it."

It seemed the only way. Sally hobbled painfully to the closet, supported by her sister's stout arm. She sank down on the closet floor and Margy closed the door and fastened it shut with the crude wooden latch. A whispered word of encouragement to her sister, and Margy, holding the baby tight, silently and swiftly passed through the back door and sped across the fields to the nearest neighbor's, a prayer in her heart for the distracted mother left alone.

Outside, the puma worried for a moment the limp body of the pup that had rashly ventured to attack the trespasser. Her new, unappeased appetite for man's blood had drawn her irresistibly back to the settlement, in spite of her intimidation of two days before. But she had approached by a circuitous route, that she might avoid a second meeting with the terrifying thing that had stalked her even while it worried its own human quarry. The puma's encounter with the lad had given her a courage unusual in her kind; in her dim understanding all men were like this one and might safely be attacked, perhaps even their lairs raided with impunity. Wherefore when the fright that frustrated her first conquest was dimmed she came arrogantly to take her toll of the once feared man creatures.

A scent new to the puma reached her nostrils and she ceased worrying the unresisting dog and drew closer to the house. The enticing kitchen odors, mingled with evidence of human occupancy that emanated from the man's den, intensified her desire. She sniffed at the door-sill, and knew that here was game worth seizing. She could find no entrance, until her eyes fell on an apparent opening a little above the ground; and instantly she sprang through the window into the house. The brittle resistance of the glass startled her, but the leap carried her through and she found herself in a singularly warm interior, with a remnant of the sash about her neck. This she clawed off, spitting and snarling at the sharp clinging thing that scratched her head spitefully before she could free herself of it.

The most engaging scent in the strange medley that smote her sensitive nose quickly drew her to the closet where the frightened woman cowered. Sally had heard with dismay the crash of the animal's entrance, and was torn between hope that the savage beast would leave her in safety and hope that it would remain long enough to permit her sister to reach the neighbor's house.

The sniffing of the panther at the lower edge of the door caused her to shrink as far back as she could in the shallow space; and as she did so a tugging at her dress chilled her blood with fresh fear. For an instant she believed the animal had inexplicably got its paw into the closet; then suddenly she understood, and her hysterical laugh of relief sent the panther with a bound to the middle of the room, snarling distrustfully.

But before Sally could pull the fold of her skirt from beneath the door where it had attracted her jailer's investigating claws, the animal, noting the motion as Sally attempted to draw it in, pounced back upon it. Clawing at the stuff and seizing it with her teeth, the panther drew it out farther and farther, and the now thoroughly frightened woman found that she was being dragged forward until she was held close against the lower part of the door, unable to help herself. Half swooning with apprehension, she feared to cry out lest her voice infuriate the beast to greater effort. Would the purchase the panther had on the stout fabric enable it to draw hard enough to break the simple wooden latch? Sally wondered in an agony of terror as the hinges creaked with the strain.

Then the animal suddenly and for no apparent reason lost interest in its endeavor. The unfamiliar material was after all a mere plaything, not related in the panther's brain to the human on the other side of the wooden wall except as an uneatable possession, and

240

she had come on a different quest. While the woman in the closet breathlessly and with renewed hope pulled her skirt carefully inch by inch back through the crack, the panther explored the room. She smelt the turkey on the table, and dragged it off with her paw. Here was a titbit the flavor of which she well knew, though unaccountably the bird had none of the bothersome feathers of those she occasionally had stolen from their roost in the trees. She fell eagerly to eating and had nearly finished it, when she raised her head to a human call that floated in through the window.

The woman heard it, too, and a new horror gripped her heart. She knew the call; it announced the return of Davie from his hunt for squirrels, and he probably would walk into the house unsuspectingly and fall a victim to the bloodthirsty intruder! The horrified mother lifted her voice to warn him, but the cry, none too strong in her weakened state, would not carry to the approaching boy. She tried to rise, that she might throw herself against the door and break it open, to brave the panther and prevent if she could the sacrifice of her child at any cost to herself. But she could not even get to her feet, and there was no way for her ·to lift from within the latch, which was operated from the outside. She heard the panther padding across the floor as if to meet the doomed lad as he entered, and with the realization of her helplessness to avert the tragedy she fell into a half-fainting apathy.

But Davie did not impetuously enter the cottage. As he came up the path the mangled form of his beloved Buster and the tracks in the snow apprized his budding woodsman's sense of a part of what had taken place. He knew the tracks, for he had studied the footprints of the panther on several occasions; and instead of fear his feeling was one of hot anger as he sorrowfully gazed at the torn remains of his old playmate. Buster had pleaded to accompany him when he went after squirrels, but the boy had sternly ordered him to remain at home and look after the women-folks and the baby. And now he had lost his life in an heroic attempt to carry out his master's instructions! At the thought Davie lifted his eyes anxiously to the house.

As he looked he saw the head of the panther rise into the broken window-frame, its narrowed green eyes contemplating him fiercely, bared teeth gleaming between snarling lips. A sickening wonder of what had happened within the room flashed into his brain, and the anger he had felt over the killing of his pet flamed higher. He raised the little twenty-two to his shoulder, aimed at the ugly visage, and fired.

The head disappeared from the window, and he could hear the animal thrashing about inside. With the confidence of youth in his aim and the power of his rifle he dashed unafraid into the house.

By great good fortune the little bullet had penetrated the brain, entering at the eye, and the big cat was twitching its last as Davie burst in.

He gloated for a moment over the tawny form that lay stretched beneath the window, and his heart swelled as full realization of what he had done came to him. Then a faint moaning caught his attention, and quickly discovering its source, he opened the closet.

"Oh, Davie boy, thank God you're safe! I thought the panther would git you," sobbed his mother as she drew him down to her. She clung to him tightly as he helped her to rise and supported her to her chair. Then in response to his excited questions she told briefly of what had occurred, and Davie ran to the back door, just in time to hallo reassuringly to his aunt and the neighbors who were running up to the house, armed with a varied collection of weapons.

His aunt laughed shrilly in her relief as her glance comprehended the scene. She turned to her young nephew.

"We could see you come up the path while we were comin' over the hill, Davie, an' we yelled to warn you. But you kept on an' disappeared under the eaves an' we reckoned we'd find you all clawed up. But I guess we need n't 've feared fer you—you with your big-

244

game rifle an' all!" she bantered. "My, what a horrid big beast! Were n't you frightened, Davie?"

"Naw!" blustered the youthful slayer, kicking the limp body contemptuously to hide his confusion. "I jest up an' shot 'im when he started to climb outer the winder. Guess if I c'n bark a squir'l I c'n hit somethin' as big as this here head!" he explained largely. And Davie helped the neighbors drag the dead panther into the woodshed.

"Well, the lad 's his pa's own son when it comes to shootin'," complacently remarked his mother, the babe held close to her breast and her eyes proudly following its valiant brother. "An' we got our wish, Margy, fer the skin's ourn. Won't the men-folks feel sheepish, though, when they git back an' find we 've bagged the game right here to home!"

"Laws-a-mercy, we ain't got any dinner fer Tom an' us all that 's fittin' to eat!" Margy cried as her eyes sought the bird they had prepared and discovered what had happened to it. She stooped and gingerly gathered up the remains of the panther's meal. "He sp'iled our Thanksgivin' dinner, that's certain, the thievin' critter!"

But Dave junior, unerring marksman, slayer of man-eating panthers, was again to the rescue. The half-dozen squirrels hanging at his belt would provide a highly appetizing substitute for roast turkey, in the form of a delicious squirrel pie; and Davie's marksmanship had saved the Thanksgiving feast as well!

Grandpa Doolittle measured the panther and announced it to stretch eight feet from nose to tip of tail. "It's a whoppin' big 'un, Davie," he said; "bigger 'n any I ever see. It'll heft nigh to two hunderd pounds, I reckon. The boys wouldn't let ye go along 'cause ye were too small, I'm told," he added, his old eyes twinkling. "Well, ye'll soon be havin' a chance to crow over them, lad."

A little later the trailing pack, having followed the scent to the cliff and there come upon a fresh track leading away from it, burst into the MacWhirter dooryard in full cry and vociferated their demands to enter the house.

THE REFUGEE

The leg-weary followers came straggling along after them, their puzzlement and anxiety over the turn in affairs growing as the trail led ever closer to their habitations.

When they caught up with the excited dogs, that were being restrained with difficulty from plunging through the windows, they were met by the gibing stay-at-homes with an amazing tale. That the quarry they sought had turned the tables upon them, invaded Dave MacWhirter's home, and been killed by a mere child, the chagrined hunters seemed loath to believe. Whereupon the jubilant Davie led them to the woodshed, where the slain refugee from the fire-swept upper country lay sprawled across the floor in stark proof—the victim of her illusions.

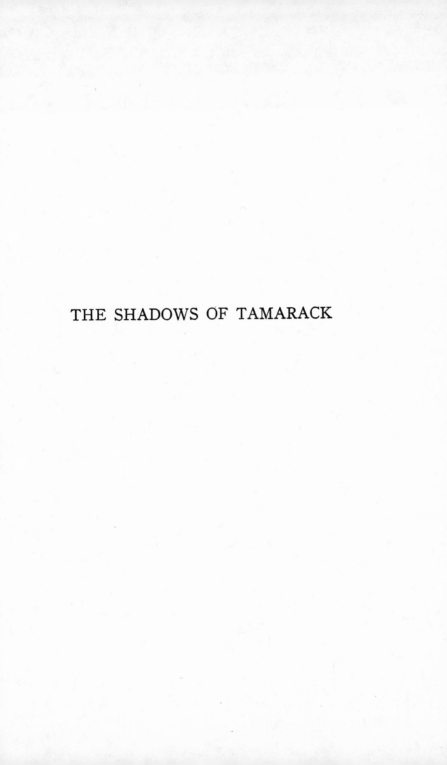

THE SHADOWS OF TAMARACK

THE SHADOWS OF TAMARACK

HEAD bent to the stinging gusts, the young backwoodsman plowed through the new-fallen snow that blanketed the pasture clearing, impatient at its hindering softness. The hard lines about his mouth and the wrathful gleam of his eyes were outward evidence of an inner turmoil that was slowly sickening his heart beyond healing. The somber forest rampart rising before him through the swirling white wreaths was no more forbidding than the black wall of distrust and angry passions that reared itself at his back, an impassable barrier towering between him and the cabin home from which he fled.

His course lay toward the farther edge of the pasture, where as he neared it the trail opening showed only as a blot of deeper gloom in the gloomy ranks of spruce and fir. The flanks of the forest that curved about the clearing seemed to draw in upon him as he ad-

251

vanced, as though impatient to gather him and his dark thoughts into their own black shadows.

For all his iron determination his step lagged as he drew closer to the forest's edge. Welling up from his heart, a longing to turn his head for one last glimpse of the little cabin at the farther limit of the clearing almost mastered him. But perversely the hard lines about his mouth tightened and the gleam of his eyes deepened as he beat down the momentary weakness with the sledge of his anger. Setting his face stiffly to the front, he mended his stride and plunged into the enveloping twilight of the wood.

As Jason Moore plodded over the back trail to the lumber camp sharp sudden reminders of his anticipations of but an hour or two before assailed him on every side. Here where the trail skirted a swamp were the broken stems of a cluster of holly from which he had torn a handful of sprays for the table; there was the giant spruce from whose deep frost-crack seaming its bole he had pried out a fragrant chunk of gum for his girl wife, Margy; here at a fallen pine he had stooped to tie a loose thong of his snow-shoe and chafed at the delay. Less than two hours since had he hurried homeward through these same silent trees; it seemed ages ago, with the tragedy that had met him instead of the joyous home-coming of his imaginings.

An unexpected halt in the work at the camp had warranted him in laying off for a few days, and he had started out long before sun-up that morning for a surprise visit home. Margy would be overjoyed, he knew, for the break in her loneliness, for this was his first parting from her since they had been married only a short year before; and his own pleasure in the occasion was no less keen. Underneath the stars that snapped and sparkled in the frosty sky among the tree-tops, through the grayness of first dawn and the succeeding rosy glow of awakened day, he had journeyed on fast-gliding snowshoes, his thoughts of the welcome at the other end of the trail making little of the long miles.

When at length he arrived just past the noon hour, his disappointment at finding the cabin so strangely deserted had chilled him. The lonely, cheerless interior mocked the anticipations that had thronged his mind during all the hard trip through the winter woods. Apparently Margy had not been in the cabin for several hours; the wood-stove was cold, and the gray ashes might have been those of the morning fire, or— A sudden fear gripped him: could she have been away for longer than since morning? Vaguely he went about the little room and the smaller bedroom, his masculine eyes unable to gain any evidence of the length of her absence. The rooms were scrupulously neat, which unreasonably gave him a dim idea that her leaving had been premeditated. This seemed to dispose of the likelihood of an accident. Cold, hungry, and dispirited, he groped in his mind for an explanation.

Many simple ones might have occurred to him, had not the specter of an old hurt risen before him with the scouting of the accident theory. He tried to banish it as unworthy, but it persisted with his growing uneasiness. A crunching of snow outside halted his thoughts, and he glanced out of the window hopefully. But it was only a distant neighbor, ax on shoulder, who was crossing the clearing. He stepped out and hailed him. If there was any news floating about that he ought to become aware of, the man might give him the clue to it.

The neighbor turned toward the open door. "Hello, Jason," he called back. "Thought you was over to the camp on the Branch. Reckon you was n't expected an' found it sort o' lonesome like in there."

"Work slacked fer a few days an' I come over fer a spell," Jason answered him. "Margy ain't to home," he offered tentatively, trying to assume a casual tone. The other grinned knowingly and nodded.

"I see her over to Lem Hankins's a spell ago. She 's—"

Whatever else he intended to tell, Jason did n't wait to hear. He interrupted with a

255

mumbled remark about the cold and turned abruptly into the cabin. The neighbor gazed a moment wonderingly at the closed door, then went his way, chuckling over the impatience of young married fellows.

Inside Jason slumped into a chair. Rage, chagrin, and hurt pride at the confirmation of his unwelcome belief battered at his soul. So Margy *had* been renewing her friendship with the man he once had feared as a rival and whom he had come to regard with cold dislike ever since he squatted over at the base of Tamarack Hill!—too near, Jason always thought, for a rejected suitor. To add to his vexation, Margy had never shown the spirit toward him that Jason considered proper. She treated him exactly as she did the few other neighbors of the thinly settled countryside, and Lem's attitude toward her was one of simple friendliness that to Jason's mind was incomprehensible. But the small seed of misgiving had not sprouted into anything really dangerous to his peace of mind until now, when it suddenly thrust out roots that twined themselves chokingly about his heart.

Forlorn of spirit he sat there, his unhappy thoughts thriving upon themselves, until slowly awakening suspicion became certainty. It was at this stage of his brooding that Margy entered the house. His haggard face arrested the surprised greeting that rose to her lips as she confronted him, cheeks rosy from the sharp, snowy air and eyes sparkling. Jason surveyed her silently for a moment as she stood before him. He saw the sudden fading of the joyous look, and his anguish of spirit deepened as he noted the change of expression. Then Margy spoke.

"Jason!" she breathed, hesitating and fearful. "Whatever's the matter? Anything happened at the camp? You look awful." She went to him and laid her hand on his shoulder.

He scowled up at her and answered harshly: "No, nothin' 's happened that you don't know about. I jest come over fer a visit."

257

Resentfully he shrugged himself away from her hand and relapsed into a sullen mood that her own manner gradually began to reflect. He would not talk, and Margy, her face now stony and set, threw off her outer garments, built a fire in the cold stove, and busied herself in getting a meal for him. The minutes passed in silence charged with an indefinable antagonism, until she bid him draw up to the table. Then as her voice broke the tension, in a burst of angry denunciation Jason unburdened his mind.

The girl, overwhelmed by the torrent of biting words, stood by the table rigidly, the kettle of tea poised over his cup, while she listened. Her eyes narrowed as he concluded, but for several moments she said nothing, and he accepted her attitude as proof of all he had charged her with. When finally she did speak it was not to explain, but only to admit defiantly that she *had* been at Lem's cabin; and Jason's reply was to spring from his seat and don his cap and mackinaw in dull rage. Flinging over his shoulder a threat never to return, he slammed the cabin door upon her startled cry of remonstrance, fastened his snowshoes to his feet with fingers that fumbled the thongs, and strode off into the rising storm.

Jason's swift progress under the stress of the tumult raging in his heart slowed somewhat as he took the rise of a hardwood ridge over which the trail led. As he ascended he could not banish from his thoughts the memory of the view this little height of land gave of his cabin. He fought down the desire to gaze back upon it as he approached the crest; he had conquered the impulse to turn his head at the clearing-limits, and so would he refrain now from any backward glance. At the end of his climb he stepped out of the timber upon the small plateau at the top—a wind-swept space bare of trees commanding broad vistas of the countryside. It came to him with a painful thrust that the trail led to this spot for just the reason that it afforded a glimpse of the snug home in which he had such pride. It was possible to cross the ridge at other points with less climbing, but he had always come this way on his occasional journeys that he might have a bird's-eye view of the little homestead.

And in the midst of his self-assurances that for once he would not look back upon it, the urge of desire deep within him overbore his reluctance and he turned in his stride for a last sight of the cabin home he had left forever. It was nearly obscured by the whirling snow, but the eyes of his memory saw its familiar outlines plainly, and a lump came into his throat as he gazed. Margy was there; what was she doing now? he wondered against his will. With the question came another slowly forming, questioning thought. Had he taken too much for granted? Perhaps—insistently the doubt forced itself upon his judgment—perhaps he had been too quick to condemn her. . . .

Over toward Tamarack a tiny moving spot of color caught his eyes and drew them to a hurrying form headed toward the cabin at its base. He could see dimly the figure that appeared and disappeared among the sparse growth of trees lining the valley, and something about it caused him to sharpen his gaze. As the figure came out into the cleared ground surrounding the log house a wandering current of air lifted for a moment the snow curtain. The clearer view confirmed his belief; it *was* she. No one else in the settlement had a red-hooded capote such as he had brought her from the Hudson's Bay post he had reached on one of his guiding-trips before they were married. His heart froze as recognition came; then the blood surged hotly back as anger such as he had never yet known took possession of him, erasing cleanly from his thoughts the slowly growing misgivings of his own conduct. His face crimsoned with the rush of emotions, and he stared stupefied with the hurt and horror of it as the speeding girl, without even the formality of knocking, entered the cabin of the man he distrusted.

"So ye'd do that!" Jason muttered grimly. "Light out fer that feller again the minute I git out o' the way! I knowed I was right in what I suspicioned. But ye'll pay fer it, the both o' ye!" A rage for vengeance upon these two who had set at naught the conventions of a Puritanic community and robbed him of home and happiness flared up within him. He would break in upon them, confronting them in their iniquity and— His fists clenched and unclenched as he half formulated the manner of his reckoning with them. As he started down the side of the ridge in the direction of Tamarack Hill, through the snowy dusk two yellow beams from a lighted lamp shot mockingly from the windows of the cabin.

Recklessly Jason took the descent, his fury driving him on regardless of the danger of tripping. Once his snowshoe caught on a stubby branch sticking up just beneath the deceptive white covering, and he plunged a-sprawl in the snow. Flounderingly he managed to get upright again, uttering hot words over the ill chance; and ignoring the torn web of the shoe, which made difficult his going, he plunged forward again toward the goal of his revengeful thoughts. Interspersed with these came fleeting memories of the quiet, simple joys of his life during the past year, and his soul writhed with the knowledge that all this had ruthlessly been taken from him. He cursed his error in leaving Margy for the job at the lumber camp, alone and in such dangerous proximity to the man who once had wanted her. But his wages for the winter's work had been needed for certain ambitious designs, in which Margy shared—with fine deceit, he now decided bitterly. Howsoever, he brooded vindictively as he drew closer to the stabbing cheeriness of the window light, since happiness had been torn from him, he soon would tear it from them, for all time.

Cold, ruthless determination succeeded his hot wrath as he neared the cabin and Margy's laugh, high and shrill and suddenly repressed, scourged his ears. He knew why she laughed, he thought, and his mouth twisted tighter in stern resolve. He would approach noiselessly, push his way in without warning, and overcome these two despoilers by the suddenness of his entry. Then—primitive justice would decide the issue.

Night was coming on as he strode up to the threshold. Just before he reached it the light suddenly went out, leaving the interior in darkness, and a door within slammed shut. Faint sounds of scuffling came to him, but no voices. Could they have become aware of his presence? He decided not; his approach had been soundless, and no face had appeared at the windows. Reaching down, he loosed the toe-holds of his snowshoes, and stepped out of them as he lifted the latch. Opening and closing the door almost in one motion, he stood in the cabin's single room, his eyes straining to penetrate the gloom. Without warning, out of the blackness a darker mass took faint outline as it rose and towered over him, and before he could arrange his faculties a savage blow descended upon his shoulder, glanced upward and spent its force on the side of his head. The terrific impact sent him crashing to the floor, unconscious, but not before a stricken yell escaped him and broke the eerie silence of the cabin.

When Jason slammed the door upon his going, Margy stood irresolute for a moment, then ran to the window from which her girlish face, white and drawn, gazed tensely at the receding figure. The unhappy emotions flaming within her had left their impress on her features, but the reborn longings that surged into her heart with his leaving were gradually smoothing out the faint, unlovely traces. When at the edge of the wood Jason's step slowed for the briefest space, her hungry eyes marked the indecision, and the quick hope that he would turn caught at her throat. Then in the next instant the snow-draped shadows blotted him from her vision, and she sank to the floor, weeping in utter misery.

"Oh, why did n't I tell him!" she sobbed. "I 'd oughter told him, 'stead of gittin' spunky an' lettin' him think what he did. But he had n't no call to say all those things afore he give me a chance to explain," she added miserably, in half-hearted self-defense. Her eyes fell on a bunch of holly and a big chunk of spruce gum thrown atop the stove-lengths in the wood-box, and this evidence of Jason's thought for her brought a fresh burst of sorrow.

After a time she stemmed the tears with her gingham apron and rose listlessly to her feet. Her forlorn gaze wandered mistily about the cozy, plain kitchen living-room of the cabin, now so suddenly become desolate. Its adornments of red-berried sprays of rowan garnered by herself from the frosty aisles of the wood flouted her dreary thoughts with their gay color. The seething kettle which she had replaced on the stove, sending up its aroma of tea, brought a poignant reminder of her futile effort to soften his mood.

As she moved over to set it aside the thought of Jason trudging through the storm—cold, hungry, and without even the comfort of the hot brew prepared for him—overwhelmed her with remorse. She yearned for a means of undoing the tragedy for which she now blamed only herself. She had driven him away by her obstinate refusal to set matters right; she must undo her fault by bringing him back—if it were not too late. Instantly her mind was made up

266

as the hope that she might still overtake him and persuade him to return grew within her.

Swallowing a cup of the bitter boiled tea, she hastily donned her heavy outdoor garments, attached the little "bear-paw" racquets to her feet and sped over Jason's now nearly obliterated trail leading into the forest. As she breasted the gale laden with stinging snow her mind questioned the possibility of coming up with him. A sob rose in her throat and was beaten back with a tearful prayer for courage and strength. In the woods the sudden comparative quiet revived her hopes, and she plodded sturdily forward on her quest through the stern, forbidding mutterings of the trees.

She had not gone far when a disturbing premonition that another presence kept pace with her impelled her to turn and gaze along the back trail apprehensively. She could discover no sign of life. But the feeling persisted, and after proceeding a short distance she turned again and stood in her tracks while she searched the pallid dusk for the cause of her uneasiness. A shadow that seemed a trifle denser than the gloom of the thickets appeared to stir. Her eyes fastened upon it intently, seeking to discover whether it was life or illusion. Suddenly she was unpleasantly enlightened.

Back in the undergrowth not far from the trail a gaunt old bear had viewed with glowering, red-rimmed eyes the two figures that glided past his place of concealment. A bad wound from a hunter's bullet had prevented his ranging to gorge on the autumn's plenitude of blueberries and mast, and he had failed to put on a blanket of fat against the long sleep; so that instead of holing up with the first cold snows he was doomed to wander miserably through the winter, seeking what scanty sustenance remained to keep life within his shaggy, hollow sides. In his ill-conditioned state he had sought shelter from the bitter wind in a copse of low-growing fir, where he lay in surly impatience for the storm to abate.

When the man appeared the bear all but dashed out upon him, to strike down the inter-

He bared his teeth in a soundless snarl of fury

loper, partly in savagery at being disturbed and partly driven by his overpowering hunger; but a strange distaste for the encounter came suddenly upon him and stayed his rush. Swaying his head in puzzled protest, he backed sullenly into his retreat and bared his teeth in a soundless snarl of fury at being balked. Perhaps some faint emanations of the angry passions seething within the fleeing human had carried a subtle warning to brute sensibilities. Whatever the reason may have been, Jason continued on his way wholly unaware of the close call.

Nursing the cruel ache at his vitals, the old bear drowsed in his cold bed until again the sound of snowshoes roused him from his lethargy. The hackles rose on his neck and he lurched to his feet to peer wrathfully through the screen of brush at the intruder who dared to return. But this was a different being who now ventured to trespass upon his misery. He waited craftily until the figure had passed by, and his courage rose with the message carried to his questioning senses; from the evidence this seemingly was quarry he could stalk with less hazard. In other than these lean times he would have faded quickly from the presence of any man creature, but starvation had overcome his prudence and he withdrew from his covert and skulked cautiously after the plodding girl. Prompted by his earlier repulse to study his victim carefully before venturing an attack, he kept to the side of the trail.

When Margy slowed her step to look behind her, the bear halted in the shadows, not yet confident enough to brave her eyes. But the meaning of her increased speed was not lost upon his wild instinct, and he quickly lessened the distance between them. When a little later Margy turned and stood facing the back trail, the old bear sensed that she was aware of being followed. He stopped and appraised her with his shrewd, twinkling little eyes, then snakily and noiselessly threaded the low growth until within a few yards of the peering figure. Rising on his hind feet his terrifying face came into Margy's view above the bushes so close that she could not stifle the gasp of frightened astonishment that rose to her lips. For a few seconds the tense situation endured; then Margy, her heart cold with fear, turned and fled. Emboldened by her precipitate flight, the bear dropped to the ground and followed at a lumbering trot.

Fleet and strong of limb, Margy seemed able for a time to maintain her lead. But where and how would the race end? The thought chilled her as she realized her predicament. The faint hope that Jason might be within earshot caused her to raise her voice in a cry for him; but no answer came. Suddenly it flashed into her fast-working brain that Lem Hankins's cabin lay only a short distance to the right. Lem, she knew, would not be at home, but if her breath and strength held out she would find safety there until he arrived. She swerved in her course and headed for the foot of Tamarack Hill.

Redoubling her exertions, Margy darted a glance over her shoulder as she reached the clearing, and was heartened to see that apparently the bear was still far enough away to enable her to reach her haven. She did not know that her escape thus far was due to the famine condition of her pursuer, whose impoverished frame was unequal to the speed of her own fresh young muscles. Reaching the cabin, she burst through the door and shut herself in with a gasping sob of thankfulness.

For a few moments she stood in the middle of the room, striving to regain her breath and listening for the approach of her pursuer. Surely she was safe here; the door was strong and the windows too high and too small to admit the bear should he attempt an entrance. He was at the door now, sniffing at the sill, and trying the stout split-planks with his paws. She shuddered as she heard the scraping of the powerful curved claws on the wood. But luckily she was no longer in danger of their cruelty, and Lem was due to return at any time and would frighten the beast away or kill him. She fortified herself with these assurances, and removing the racquets from her feet, groped for the matches; a light would bring an added sense of security. Finding them, she set the crude coal-oil lamp to burning, and the cheeriness of it strengthened her courage.

The sniffings and scrapings around the base logs continued for some time as the besieger pursued his quest for a means of reaching the human within. Then for a space there was silence. Could he have become disheartened and gone away? Margy strained her ears for some sign of his presence; the ominous quiet was becoming more nerve-racking than the previous sounds. She tiptoed to the rear window for a look outside. As she pressed her face against the glass, a fierce head with long white teeth gleaming in a yawning red cavern of a mouth rose on the other side, and the bloodshot eyes of the bear glared into hers with horrid intentness. For several seconds Margy was held fascinated by the evilly grinning mask. Then as the staring eyes wavered before the disconcerting human gaze, she covered her face with her hands and a peal of hysterical laughter burst from her lips.

It was quickly choked back when a creaking of boards close by brought her to her senses.

She turned hastily toward the sound and trembled with fresh fear as she saw the small rear door beside the window slowly giving inward. Why had she not thought of the frailty of this, and reinforced it? While she watched, terror-stricken, the wooden hasp snapped under the pressure, and the door was pushed open. The bear's head appeared; his sinister, shifting glance fell on the girl, and the ungainly black body squeezed through. In the face of this immediate danger Margy gathered her wits. Her mind, groping distractedly for a way of escape, of a sudden remembered the tiny lean-to, used by Lem for storage purposes, that was entered through a small, tight door beside the fireplace. She stepped quickly to the table as the bear entered, snatched up the lamp, and swinging it before her, backed toward this last refuge. The bear shambled after her, but daunted by the menace of that strange waving flame, delayed his rush. Margy felt behind her for the latch, lifted it, and kicked the door open. She slipped through and shut herself within the cramped windowless cubbyhole; and setting the lamp on the earth floor sank down beside it shivering in reaction.

Would the inch of pine resist the bear's onslaught? She looked about for something to place against it, but there was no heavy object among the litter. Her searching eyes fell on an old rusted single-shot rifle that lay on wooden pegs driven into the logs, and the sight brought a flicker of hope to her. She took it down and opened the breech. A cartridge was in the chamber! One sorry bullet against that hulking black demon! But she clutched the weapon gratefully; it was her sole chance of deliverance should the animal succeed in tearing down the barrier.

Abruptly the clawing at the planks ceased and her straining ears heard the quick opening and closing of the front door, then quiet. Could it be Lem? She was puzzled by the strangeness of his entry. Before she could decide to cry a warning, a yell shattered the weird silence and was followed by the thudding of a body to the floor. She was sure of the voice. It was Jason's!

Instantly Margy swept aside her wonder over this and swung open the lean-to door. The light streamed out upon the floor of the cabin. The bear, growling over the unconscious form that lay beneath his mauling paws, turned toward her menacingly. Bringing the rifle to her shoulder, Margy aimed at the ugly visage and pressed the trigger. The narrow walls gave back a deafening crash and the concussion jarred out the light; and Margy stood half stunned for an instant in the darkness, the rifle still held at her shoulder.

Only a gurgling, gasping sigh and the floundering of a huge body succeeded the noise; then this subsided. Margy remained frozen in her position for anxious moments, her heart pounding with apprehension over the outcome. If her aim had not been true, there would be no hope for either Jason or herself. Unless the bullet had penetrated the brain, in the cramped space of the cabin the ferocity of the wounded bear would make short work of his two defenseless enemies. But no further sound came to her ears. After waiting for what seemed an age, Margy took heart over the apparent success of her shot. Cautiously she felt her way along the wall, secured matches, and retracing her steps entered the lean-to and lighted the lamp.

Its rays fell on the big, furry bulk stretched motionless on the floor, stone dead, and beside it the prone, inert figure of her husband. With a long-drawn breath blended of relief and dread she knelt beside him, all her present anxiety centered on the nature of his hurts. The swing of the bear's powerful forearm had ripped the coat from Jason's shoulder and torn a gash in his scalp. She managed to turn him on his back, the better to find if his heart still beat, and as she did so a groan came from his lips. Tears of thankfulness sprang to Margy's eyes at this evidence that he lived, and she busied herself with restoring him to consciousness. At last Jason opened his eyes and looked blankly up at her as she washed the blood from his head. She smiled down at him through her tears.

"Oh, Jason, thank God you ain't hurt as

bad as I feared," cried Margy, fervently. "I thought the bear had maybe killed you." Deftly she started to dress the cut with what facilities were at hand, awaiting his full return to understanding before saying more.

Pain, bewilderment, and gradually dawning sense mingled in Jason's haggard eyes. He struggled to a sitting posture with Margy's help, and gazed about him dazedly. His wound was only superficial, and shortly the effect of the bear's blow wore off. Slowly partial comprehension entered his brain. With returning memory he bent a questioning, accusing look on the girl who was tenderly ministering to him. Before he could voice his thoughts Margy was pouring out her story.

"I went after you, Jason. I was dreadful mean to you, over to home. I might 've explained easy, but I got mad an' let you go thinkin' I was jest no-account. Then I follered to get you to come back. A big cross bear took after me an' I run in here to get away from him. He broke in, an' I hid in the lean-to. Then some one come in quick like, an' afore I had time to cry out I heared a yell an' a fall. Then I knew 't was you, an' I opened the door an' shot the varmint with Lem's old rifle.

"I 'm mortal sorry I 'm to blame fer all this trouble, Jason. Won't you listen till—"

Jason's eyes were boring into hers during the recital, and she broke down and sobbed before their unforgiving hardness.

"You were mighty spunky to shoot the bear," he interrupted brokenly, "but you . . . you been comin' here to Lem Hankins's right along—" The old anger and hopelessness came back to him and choked his utterance. He rose unsteadily to his feet and swayed over the huddled girl, who was vainly trying to regain control of her outraged nerves. Taxed sorely by the long ordeal through which she had passed, she was brought by Jason's harsh manner to the verge of hysterics, and could offer no reply to his unspoken question.

While she struggled to fight back the weakness a jingle of sleigh-bells fell faintly on their ears. Margy raised her head quickly, and as she listened a wave of relief crossed her face.

Her sobbing ceased and she sprang to her feet as the sound grew louder and a horse drawing a pung floundered through the snow of the clearing and drew up to the cabin. Jason stood gazing out upon the new arrivals in puzzlement. Margy seized his arm.

"You hain't give me a chance to explain," she sorrowfully accused him. "Now there won't be any time, but in a minute you'll understand why—"

She dragged the sullen, wondering Jason through the doorway. The pung had stopped, and in the scant illumination they saw Lem Hankins helping out of it a heavily wrapped young woman, whom he led up to the door. His countenance lighted as he recognized the two standing at his threshold. Their faces were in half shadow and disclosed nothing unusual to the newcomers.

"Hello, Jason!" Lem called out heartily; and stepped up and wrung the hand that stretched forth reluctantly at Margy's secret urging. "Now I call this real neighborly of ye," he exclaimed, moved by the apparent friendliness of Jason's presence. "Margy, ye never told me ye had it all fixed fer you an' Jason to greet us. I take it kindly that ye both come over. Lisbeth," he introduced the blushing girl at his side, "this here 's Jason Moore and Margy; I told ye 'bout her fixin' up the cabin fer us while I been away. I reckon ye did n't know till ye got back from the camp, Jason, that I 'd gone over to Swiftwater Forks to git married, an'—"

He stopped, agape, as he spied the alien tenant of his domicile sprawled across the puncheons, its filmed eyes leering at them in the flickering lamplight. Lisbeth uttered a little scream, and clung closer to her husband's arm, which he passed protectingly about her. The dismay of the bridal pair over this other welcoming guest was ludicrous; and despite the lingering ache at her heart Margy's laughter rang out.

She too was clinging to her husband's arm, and she pinched it warningly when she saw mirrored on his features the emotions that flooded his soul as the innocent facts became clear to him. Shame, contrition, humility, pride—all were writ there legibly, though only for his wife to read, while his eyes met hers with a mute look beseeching forgiveness. The other two, in their astonishment at what their own eyes beheld, were oblivious of this ending of a domestic tragedy. Jason's tongue-tied, chastened manner was not noticed by them in the excitement.

Margy tightened her grasp on Jason's arm by way of answer to his silent pleading.

"That there's our weddin'-gift," she addressed the newly married couple gaily, "a fine, big black bear robe. We brought it to you on the hoof, in a way o' speakin', so's the groom could sup'rintend the dressin' of it."

A babel of voices arose, questioning, marveling, explaining—with reservations—and the four young people trooped into the cabin and fell to examining the stark intruder.

"An' now Lisbeth an' I'll get the weddin'

supper while you two men-folks drag that ugly present of ourn out o' the front parlor," Margy interposed; and flew happily to the task of building a fire in the cold stove.